Kirsten tried to sound offhand. 'Next time, if there is one, I'll be more careful who I offer my heart to.' She wrinkled her nose. 'Do I sound sentimental and out of date?'

'Yes, you do,' was his abrupt, surprising answer. 'In my experience, women keep their hearts firmly where nature put them. If they give anything away, it's usually their sensuality, and that for money. To the highest bidder.'

His experience, Kirsten decided, had obviously left him badly bruised. He must, she guessed, have loved very deeply the woman who had chosen his brother instead of himself.

TAKE THIS WOMAN

BY

LILIAN PEAKE

MILLS & BOON LIMITED
ETON HOUSE   18-24 PARADISE ROAD
RICHMOND   SURREY   TW9 1SR

First published in Great Britain 1988 by Mills & Boon Limited

© Lilian Peake 1988

Australian copyright 1988 Philippine copyright 1988 This edition 1988

ISBN 0 263 75960 1

Set in English Times 10 on 11 pt. 01–0488–44234

Typeset in Great Britain by JCL Graphics, Bristol

Printed and bound in Great Britain by Collins, Glasgow

CHAPTER ONE

WHEN Kirsten became personal assistant to Lennard Hazelton, never in her wildest dreams did she foresee that one day she would inherit his twenty-roomed house.

'You've been an attentive and kindly young woman, Kirsten,' he said in his bright and lively way towards the end of his ninety-five-year lifespan. 'You've been efficient and hard-working and much more of a great-niece to me—I can't say daughter, because my dear late wife was never able to give me children—than any of my younger brother's or sister's offspring. Or their offspring. So I'm leaving you the house and garden.

'When I'm gone——' here Kirsten had shaken her head '—I can't live for ever, you know—I'm trusting you to look after Tall Trees and care for it as you've looked after me and my affairs for the five or so years you've worked for me. Eighteen, weren't you, when I gave you the job?'

Kirsten had nodded, overwhelmed by Mr Hazelton's generous decision. Then she had shaken her head. 'Please leave me out of it, Mr Hazelton. Your brother and sister and their families might be very angry, and I should hate to be the centre of a family feud.'

'What I do with my property is my affair, my dear,' he had said firmly, tugging at his neatly trimmed beard, 'and the family can eat their hearts out. They'll be well provided for. But this place is going to be yours. And if they do descend on you and try to do their worst,' he had smiled, 'then I'm sure you can take on all comers. And win!'

Now, wandering round the extensive gardens, wind-tossed and a little on the wild side, she remembered Mr Hazelton's words. Looking up at the house with wonder, Kirsten could scarcely believe that she really was its owner. Lennard Hazelton had made the gesture out of the kindness of his heart. The extensive estate which surrounded it he had left to someone else.

'Mr Hazelton also provided you with a sum of money, Miss Ingram,' Philip Phipps the lawyer had told her the day he had called her in to inform her of her inheritance. 'It's not large, but in the absence of any other source of cash in your possession for care and maintenance——?'

He had waited, brows uplifted.

'None at all,' she supplied worriedly.

'Quite,' he went on, as if he had anticipated her answer. 'Which means the money, although not a fortune, should be of some real assistance to you.'

'That was very good of him,' Kirsten responded. ' "Not large", you said?' She frowned, the responsibilities of owning such a place dawning on her at last. 'I wonder if Mr Hazelton realised that there are repairs crying out to be done. You see,' she went on, 'most of the rooms need redecorating, for a start. I was in the middle of getting quotes for that when Mr Hazelton——'

'Left us,' Mr Phipps nodded. 'I'm afraid, Miss Ingram, that I can't help you there. He left this letter,' he held it up and it was in an envelope clearly marked, 'Strictly Private', 'to a great-nephew of his. Er——' he read out the name '—a Mr Scott Baird, has an address in London, it seems. Lennard Hazelton——' Mr Phipps put the letter down. 'I feel I should tell you.'

For such a forthright man, it seemed to Kirsten that he was curiously hesitant.

'He has left the house and its contents to you,' the lawyer went on, 'plus the gardens that surround the property, but,' he shuffled through the file of papers, 'he left the orchard adjacent to the gardens and the remainder of the estate—that is, the woodland, the three farms, the fields and a number of cottages in the village—to his great-nephew,' he picked up the 'Strictly Private' letter and flapped the air with it, 'Mr Scott Baird, grandson of his sister, Audrey. He——' The lawyer gave a quick, dismissing smile, glancing at his watch. 'Miss Ingram, Mr Baird is the one with the money. He's a banker, plus many other things in the City of London. I'll give you his address.'

Mr. Phipps scribbled on a sheet of paper. 'All I can suggest is that you write to him explaining the situation, and ask him for financial assistance in refurbishing the interior of the property you now own. This letter—naturally, I don't know what it contains—will be sent on to him as soon as I hear that he is back in this country from his travels abroad.'

A brief nod, another parchment-like smile, and Kirsten was sent politely but firmly on her way.

That had been more than a week ago. Since then, Mr Phipps had, at the expense of Mr Hazelton's estate—the money he had left for tying up loose ends, as he had put it—employed a surveyor to look over Tall Trees and give his verdict.

The sum of money which the surveyor had estimated would need to be spent on the property—some of which, he had said, could only be described as tumbledown—had made Kirsten reel back in horror.

'There's no way,' she had told Mr Phipps on the telephone, 'that I'll ever be able to find that kind of cash. What can I *do,* Mr Phipps?'

'You could try to raise a mortgage from a bank, Miss Ingram,' he had answered with a sigh, 'provided that you caught your bank manager in a good mood one morning.' For Mr Phipps, Kirsten thought angrily, that was a joke, but at that moment she did not find it very funny. 'But in the poor condition that place is in, I can't personally hold out much hope for the granting of this.'

'The trouble is,' Kirsten had pointed out, 'that it's my home. Mr Hazelton allowed me to live here, rent-free. It was convenient, he said, to have me living on the premises, because he often worked odd hours, sleeping in the daytime, sometimes, owing to his great age. He wouldn't have to worry, he said, about my going home alone late at night.'

'It's more *your* home than ever now, Miss Ingram,' Mr Phipps agreed reasonably. Then he let out a long sigh. 'I can only repeat my advice to you earlier. That is, to contact Mr Baird——'

'Thank you, Mr Phipps,' Kirsten had broken in, 'I might do just that.'

But, for some inexplicable reason, she did not want to. Something—intuition, maybe—told her that if Mr Hazelton's great-nephew entered her life, it would be turned upside-down. After all, if he held the purse-strings, he could call whatever tune he liked, couldn't he?

For just a few minutes Kirsten wished her life could return to the uncomplicated pattern it had followed while her employer had been alive. Nothing, she knew, would ever be the same again.

Her parents, from their modest North Country home, had been pleased for her inheritance, and sympathetic about her difficulties, but, as Kirsten well knew, her father's salary as a local government employee was just sufficient to supply them with the necessities of life, and the exceptional luxury of a package holiday, her younger sister being still of school age, with further and possibly higher education soon to come.

Since Kirsten's own income had dried up, she was forced now to live on her savings, and those were not large.

The day would come, she reflected, entering the library and realising that every single volume there belonged to her now, when even her own small stockpile of money would have vanished without trace.

Once a week, Cherry Marston from the village nearly a mile away came in to clean and tidy the place. In Lennard Hazelton's time she had come every day, but Kirsten had explained—and Cherry, with two young children and a farm-worker husband, had quite understood—how her money situation had altered since their employer had died.

Privately, Kirsten wondered how long she herself would be able to afford the luxury of having domestic help even for one day a week. For the moment, she found herself busy with all the different aspects involved in running her late employer's estate, and that few hours' help was indispensable.

Sitting at her desk one morning, she reflected with some surprise that, in carrying on her work, she was in fact doing so without pay, for the unknown Scott Baird.

The postman's small red van came to a gravelly stop in the sweeping drive outside the front entrance. As he sped away, Kirsten collected the post. Most of it was, as usual, for her late employer. These she would have to go through and inform the senders of the changed circumstances. There was, however, one letter for her.

Pushing it to the bottom of the pile, she went through the others and mentally wrote answers to many of them even before she opened them, since they announced from which sections of authority and from which specific companies they came.

Putting them aside at last, she slit open the long, rather important-looking letter addressed to herself. At the top was the name and logo of a well known and internationally established firm of property developers. Bemused, she read the letter's contents, felt her cheeks turn white, then red, and reached for her chair at the desk.

'We understand,' the letter said, 'that your house, Tall Trees, is about to be put on the market for sale. May we state from the start our great interest in your particular property? We would be prepared to offer you a substantial sum for the house. If you yourself have a figure in mind, please do not hesitate to tell us, and we would be prepared to match it with an offer of our own. Assuring you of our best intentions . . .'

No, no! was Kirsten's first reaction to the very idea of selling Mr Hazelton's residence, which in his lifetime he had loved so much. Then she wondered how the company had been so badly misinformed as to her intentions. Of course she wouldn't sell the house. How could Mr Phipps—he was the only person she could think of who might have tried to help her, as he thought, in this way—have assumed she would even consider selling? And to a property developer too!

It took her only a few minutes to type a reply, then she raced down the hill on her bicycle to catch the morning's collection in the village and pedalled determinedly back to the house to carry on with her work.

The weather was fine for a change, the early spring sun shining directly into the large room in which she had worked with Mr Hazelton. He had liked, he once said, to see her bent over her work with the sun shining on her lovely young face and her rich brown hair. The colour had reminded him so much of his wife's when he had first met her.

'I may be an old man, Kirsten,' he had mused once, 'but there's still a strong streak of romance in me. Don't ever let anyone try to persuade you that, as a man ages, so the poetry in his soul dies away.'

Kirsten had smiled, nodding. 'It's the same for ladies, too,' she had told him. 'Or so my grandmother told me.

She said she might be approaching eighty, but in her heart she still felt like a girl of twenty.'

Lennard had nodded, understanding perfectly. Now, the late March sun picked out unsuspected auburn lights in Kirsten's dark hair. Its glow illuminated her features as she concentrated on the letters she was answering, informing the correspondents that, for as long as possible, and until she received further instructions, she would carry on dealing with the late Mr Hazelton's affairs.

The double glass doors leading to the stone terrace at the rear of the house were thrown open to welcome the unseasonable mildness. Birds sang and darted over shrubs and bushes that flourished just outside the large room. In the summer, the house was reasonably warm and dry, but living in the place as she had been, Kirsten knew that, in the winter months, and even the early spring, it was a different story.

The dampness which was in the air whenever it rained or snowed, or when November mists descended, penetrated through all the twenty rooms of the house, and made her shiver even in her own bedroom, in spite of the warmth thrown out by the roaring fires that crackled in the old-fashioned grates. The house was so large, the sketchy form of central heating which Mr Hazelton had had installed simply could not cope.

Something brought Kirsten's head round. There was a movement like a rustle from the direction of the garden. When a man appeared on the balustraded terrace, framed by the wide doorway, she felt a scream rise, but stifled it.

He was broad and strongly built, with shoulders that looked as if they could carry a load of troubles with ease, other people's as well as his own.

His thick black hair had been fingered by the breeze, the set of his mouth having a don't-argue-with-me look about it. But it was the deep brown of his eyes, watchful and enigmatic, that hit a responsive chord inside her, bringing a tingle to her nervous system and a faint touch of moisture to the palms of her clenched hands.

No man before had made such an impact at first sight. While she felt the pull of his magnetic field drawing her to him, a saner voice bleeped out an emergency warning telling her not to touch. Danger! A million volts!

Yet, when he spoke, his tone was so reasonable, Kirsten wondered what the cautioning side of her was talking about.

'You're—Miss Ingram?' The hesitation told her that he was surprised. The inflection in his voice told her also that he was in the habit of using it to influence others and swing them round to his point of view. *I'm not in the market for persuasion*. The thought sprang to her mind from out of nowhere.

He looked down at the step into the room, but did not take it. 'I rang the front door bell, but no one came, so I assumed the place was empty.' He added, as if it were important, 'I came in through the gate from the orchard.'

Kirsten had not yet adjusted to the fact that Cherry Marston was not around as much as she used to be, answering bells, both door and telephone. 'I was working,' she answered. 'Sorry I didn't hear. Who——?'

'Scott Baird, great-nephew of the late Lennard Hazelton. Maybe you've heard of my existence. I don't carry an identity picture, but I do have a card——' he raked in the pocket of his zipped jacket '—somewhere in here.'

Out of politeness, Kirsten took it. She already believed him, having traced a likeness, faint though it was, to Mr Hazelton—in the positive statement of his nose, the long-jawed face, the squared, determined chin. But a glance at the card told her something that she did not know—that Scott L Baird was one of the directors of a group of international bankers. Yes indeed, Mr Phipps, she thought, how right you were when you told me that Scott Baird was the one with the money!

Looking up at him, she smiled. 'I've certainly heard about you,' she declared. 'You're the man who's as good as made me into a female hermit living on an island.' At his puzzled glance, she added, 'I own the house and garden, whereas everything else around it is yours.'

Again he looked at the step. 'Mind if I join you on that island? Or would you consider it trespassing if I came over the threshold?'

Kirsten laughed, but, she told herself, it was not only at the joke he had made. It was because of the wonderful feeling that was chasing round her veins, the strange lightness of her heart that the man's presence was giving her. 'Please come in,' she managed, in spite of her curious and sudden breathing problem.

As they faced each other, their eyes locked and Kirsten knew she had to say something to break the tension. 'I'm afraid I trespass every time I go out of the garden and through the gate into the orchard—your orchard. It's the quick way to the main road, you see.'

He smiled and her heart began to bump. 'I think,' he answered, 'we can bend the law a bit to allow that.'

She nodded, wishing her breathing would return to normal. Looking around, she wondered what to do with him, and wondering also why he had come.

He was in the room now and his eyes rested on her thoughtfully. 'Could I persuade you,' he looked around him, 'to show me round my late great-uncle's house? It's some years since I visited him. I'd like to refresh my memory. After all, as you say, the land my great-uncle left me encloses your property, so that in itself calls for some measure of give and take between us.' His brows lifted in an amused kind of way. 'Don't you agree?'

'Oh yes,' she answered, 'I certainly agree.' I would, she thought bemusedly, agree to anything this man suggested—almost. He had that look about him, and there was something that came from within him that made him practically irresistible to a woman—this woman anyway, Kirsten thought, wishing her heartbeats would return to normal. Was this man really so special that he had, within a few minutes of meeting him, knocked her emotional balance sideways?

She thought of Robin, of whom she was very fond—being with him made her feel pleasantly happy, but he had never had this breath-robbing effect on her lungs, even when he was kissing her.

For some reason, despite the sunshine slanting in through whatever window it could find, the house with Scott Baird at her side looked just that bit shabbier than she had judged it to be. She was, she decided, seeing it not with her eyes, but his.

Few faults passed his scrutiny, his quick glance picking out the peeling paint here, the patchy, discoloured wallpaper there; the warped internal doors to some of the rooms, the broken window-panes in one or two of the downstairs areas.

She had, in the past, tried to tell Mr Hazelton that the house was showing its age. He had listened carefully to her list of repairs, the modernisation that cried out to be done, if only to preserve the outer fabric of the place, let alone its interior.

He had nodded and said, 'Tell me about it in a couple of months, Kirsten, when I've had time to consult my accountant. I've a feeling that my capital is diminishing fast, and if it comes to a choice,' he had smiled brightly at her, 'I would rather do without those modern touches than be forced to do without you.'

Kirsten knew now, through Mr Phipps, that Lennard Hazelton's fortune had, at that time, actually been increasing. This money had been distributed generously among his relatives. In leaving the house to her, she reasoned, he had quite overlooked the fact that the place would require a great deal of cash to maintain it at its present level of repair, let alone cover the cost of the increasingly necessary repairs. The amount of money he had actually allocated, although thoughtful on his part, was quite insufficient compared with the sum that would eventually be needed.

Scott's face assumed a slight frown which deepened as he went from room to room. Was he, she wondered, as puzzled as she was as to how she would be able to maintain it into the future?

'It's very large, isn't it?' she commented in an attempt to discover his true opinion of the place.

As he stood across from her in the main bedroom, his brows almost touched in two curves of doubt. 'You live here?' he asked at last.

Kirsten nodded. 'It's been my home for over six years now.'

'Don't you feel—lonely?'

She shook her head. Strangely, she hadn't—until this man had asked the question.

The extension telephone rang on a table near the window. 'Please excuse me,' she said, and he moved to allow her to pass him. Answering it, she smiled brightly. 'Robin? Hi, I've missed you. It's over ten days, isn't it, since you phoned?' It was a question that really needed no answer, so she went on, 'Are you coming over for the weekend? How much longer are they going to keep you in Holland?'

'Kirsten.' Robin halted. His breathing sounded a little strangled. 'I've something to—to tell you. But I don't quite know how.' He paused again. There seemed to be someone in the room with him, even standing beside him, judging by the whispers. 'There's a girl—her name's Paula. Well, she and I——'

Kirsten felt herself go cold. 'Don't—don't go on, Rob,' she choked. 'I understand—I really do.' But I don't, she told herself. How could he have misled me so during all those other phone calls from the other side of the Channel? He had been there working on a project for his firm for nearly three months now. 'How long have you known?'

'Well, to be honest, almost from the time I came out here. We met a couple of weeks after.'

Which was even before Mr Hazelton had died, Kirsten calculated, before she had known the house had been left to her. Since becoming its owner, she had even visualised Robin and herself living there after they had married, finding a job while Robin carried on with his, earning sufficient between them to keep the place going.

'Right, Robin,' she said as briskly as she could manage. 'That's surely long enough for you to discover she's got something I haven't. I—I wish you luck, Rob, both of you . . .'

'Kirsten, I——'

'Don't give it another thought.' Kirsten crossed her fingers and hoped her voice would not crack. ''Bye, Rob. See you around, maybe.'

Her hand was slow in replacing the receiver. It would have to be shaking, she thought, and in front of this stranger too. It would have to happen with him looking on, pity filling his eyes.

Turning to the window, she stared out. All right, she rationalised, so she hadn't been madly in love with

Robin, but they had spent a couple of happy years together, meeting whenever Mr Hazelton had been able to spare her. Too much is happening, she thought, too many changes compressed into too short a period . . .

Taking a breath to calm herself, she thought, desperately trying to reason herself into accepting the break-up, thinking, that's life. Then the breath turned into a shattering sob.'

Covering her face with her hand, she muttered, 'I'm sorry about this, please excuse me,' and made for the door.

A strong arm came out, halting her. She tried to shake free, but it pulled her round and she found herself up against a wall of body, a very male one. Its chest was hard, the shoulders wide, and one of them suddenly became a kind of hard-packed cushion on her cheek. An arm like iron held her close, steadying her shoulders as she cried, while a hand seemed to be busy stroking her hair.

Although he was, strictly speaking, a complete stranger, there was something about the solid frame of him, with its tough muscular filling that made her feel she had known him all her life. Which was ridiculous, she thought, since they had only just met.

'I can take a guess as to how you feel,' he was saying, and even the vibration of his voice, mixing with the strong beat of his heart, sounded soothing.

It took a few moments for the sincerity in his tone to reach her through her sobs. She eased away, uncaring that her eyes would be puffy and waterlogged. 'Why?' she asked unbelievingly. 'You mean that *you've* had the brush-off at some time in your life?'

His smile brought a transformation to his face and a curious quicksilver sensation to her nervous system. It had smoothed away the creases above his nose, the frown marks which told of an impatience and a short fuse with fools. It softened the line of his mouth, too, which Kirsten did not doubt could deliver verbal blows to any careless subordinate in that international bank of his, or any other creature who had the audacity to cross him.

'What makes you think,' he queried with amusement, 'that I'm immune from emotional upheavals? I'm only human.'

Kirsten moved away, using the clean white square he had offered her. 'It's just that with your——' looks, she had been going to say, 'your——' physique, she had been intending to add, but both words seemed too personal. After all, she reasoned, she had known the man less than an hour, despite the fact that he had held her so protectively in his arms.

'My——?' he queried, amused again.

'Commanding presence,' she managed at last, 'I would have thought that no woman would dare refuse whatever you asked.'

He laughed then, his head going back, but he sobered quickly. 'There was a woman: I offered her marriage. So did my elder brother, and he won. At the time, his bank balance was larger than mine.'

So the experience had turned him cynical? And he was implying that he had no permanent lady in his life? So why, she asked herself, should the thought that he was free give her this feeling of relief?

She held out the handkerchief. 'I'll wash it,' she told him, but he slid it into his trouser pocket. Pushing back her hair, she knew her face was still flushed with emotion. He watched her hand, presumably to check on whether it was still shaking. It was, she knew, as steady as a rock. Which, she reflected, must mean something, although what that 'something' was, she did not at that moment bother to work out.

'How much more of the house,' she queried, 'would

you like to see?' She smiled. 'It sounds as if I'm trying to sell you the place, doesn't it? Which,' she added hastily, 'I certainly am not.'

Downstairs again, and back in the study, he peeled off his jacket, spreading it round the back of a chair. Kirsten saw then how much its fabric had softened the feel of his shoulder against her face.

'Feeling better now?' he asked, folding his arms across his chest and looking down at her from his considerable height.

'Yes, thanks.' She gave a rueful smile. 'I'll survive.'

'Were you,' he asked in a polite tone, 'planning to marry your boyfriend?'

'We hadn't talked seriously about it, but I suppose it was in the back of our minds. But,' she lifted her shoulders and Scott Baird's eyes were drawn to them, his gaze moving down her shape, then back to her face, 'you know what they say about all those other fish in the sea?' She tried to sound offhand. 'Next time, if there is one, I'll be more careful who I offer my heart to.' She wrinkled her nose. 'Do I sound sentimental and out of date?'

'Yes, you do,' was his abrupt, surprising answer. 'In my experience, women keep their hearts firmly where nature put them. If they give anything away, it's usually their sensuality, and that for money. To the highest bidder.'

His experience, Kirsten decided, had obviously left him badly bruised. He must, she guessed, have loved very deeply the woman who had chosen his brother instead of himself.

'I'm sorry you feel that way about women.' She followed the faded pattern on the carpet with her sandalled foot. His eyes descended too, and he seemed to find her ankle interesting. Or, she wondered, was he seeing the worn patches in the carpet pile? 'Money has never played a very important part in my life,' she added, then frowned at the shabbiness around her, lifting her eyes and tracing the yellowing marks of dampness on the ceiling. 'Until now. I'm beginning to see that it has its uses.'

'Scott Baird's the one with the money,' Mr Phipps had said. 'All I can suggest is that you ask him for assistance.'

Now she eyed the man standing a few paces from her. Ask *this* man for assistance? Was it her imagination, she wondered, or had the lines around his mouth deepened, his lips grown more compressed, his brown eyes darkened? His whole face hardened. Where, she thought, was the man who had offered her sympathy, a shoulder to cry on?

'So you wouldn't refuse if I made an offer for this house?'

Kirsten gasped. 'You think I'd *sell* Tall Trees?'

He could not have missed the horror in her eyes. All the same, he named a figure which secretly staggered her. It was, she was certain, out of all proportion to its real value. He seemed to take her silence as a refusal, since he immediately increased the amount.

Kirsten began shaking her head, trying to convey to him that she would not sell the place if he offered her a fortune, but he cut into her silent indignation.

'You're a hard nut to crack, Miss Ingram,' he said sharply. 'Under that fetching exterior, you must have a heart of stone. So I'll add another five thousand.'

'Thank you, but *no!*' she almost shouted. 'I've never had any intention of selling. Whatever gave you the idea? I even had a letter from a firm of property developers— Samson Developments—asking me to sell to them. They wanted to build here, or so they implied, but I wrote back at once, telling them they could go to——'

The thought hit her so hard, she felt herself swaying. Scott Baird owned the land around Tall Trees. Supposing he was willing to sell that land, leaving her property isolated and alone, a fine old house in a sea of concrete and brick, creeping up to the very edge of her garden, fencing her in? Even though she was the owner, once they had got planning permission, there would be absolutely nothing she could so about it!

Since he did not seem surprised at her announcement, she asked, 'Have you had a letter from them too?'

'From Samson Developments? I know about their plans.'

'Plans? How could they have plans? I haven't agreed to sell. Unless——' her voice dropped to a whisper '—you have?'

He did not answer.'

'Have you, Mr Baird?'

He still did not answer the question. 'If you sold to me, Miss Ingram, the whole estate would be treated with more thought and artistry. I'd do my best to respect my great-uncle's wishes——'

'Which were to keep the house in the family!'

'Are *you* family, Miss Ingram?' His raised eyebrows mocked and irritated.

Needing the support of a chair, Kirsten sat down. It was obvious, she thought, that she had a fight on her hands. But how could she fight him—the one man who could help her financially? The house needed thousands spent on it, otherwise it would be in ruins before many years had passed.

'If—if Robin and I had stayed together,' she said slowly, gathering her thoughts, 'we would have lived here. Now, everything's changed.'

Scott Baird took the chair opposite Kirsten. 'So?'

'So,' she shook her head, trying to clear it, 'I'll have to make other plans.' She thought fast. 'I might follow up one of Mr Hazelton's pet schemes. If I hadn't been around, he said, to leave the place to, he would have turned it into a country home for senior citizens like himself.' Mr Hazelton's words were coming back to her. 'With small, self-contained apartments. Yes,' her eyes brightened at the prospect, 'that's what I'll do. Then I'd be fulfilling one of his dearest wishes.' She threw him a challenging look. Beat that, it said.

'You think you'd get a bank loan, Miss Ingram, to make your dream come true? That idea of yours——'

'Mr Hazelton's.'

'—would swallow up a small fortune.' He shook his head. 'In my eyes, the place is too far gone for such a scheme. No bank manager——'

'And you know all about banks, don't you?' she tossed at him.'

He was not put out by her sarcasm. 'It's my job, after all,' he pointed out mildly. His smile was so full of charm, her heart reeled under it, but with a self-discipline she didn't know she had, she disguised the effect he was having on her.

She returned his smile with a honey-sweet one of her onw. 'If—*if* I were to change my mind, Mr Baird, and sell this house to you, what would you do with it?' His eyes narrowed at the leading question, but he chose not to answer it. 'Would you carry out those structural repairs, call in a firm of interior decorators, modernise it, install a more up-to-date heating system?'

After a long pause, he answered, 'I couldn't make any such promise. First,' he counted on his fingers, leaning forward in his chair, 'I'd think about its possible uses—as a family residence.' He shook his head. 'Far too big for the modern family. And too expensive for your average family man, anyway. Second, what the land area it occupies could be used for.'

'You don't mean,' Kirsten broke in, 'you'd knock it down?'

'Bulldoze is the word you want.'

'I do not want! Mr Hazelton's dearest wish was to keep it as it is—'

Scott frowned. 'I saw a copy of my great-uncle's will. I don't remember any statement or request to that effect.'

'He told me over and over——'

'How often did you take my great-uncle by the arm, Miss Ingram, and show him round his own crumbling residence?'

'He wasn't able to make the stairs for quite a few years before he died. He wouldn't even consider installing a stair-lift so he could get up to the next floor. He slept downstairs.'

'Therefore,' Scott returned, eyes glinting like a lawyer who was scoring points against an opponent, 'he never saw the dilapidated state of the place, how some of it has deteriorated almost beyond saving. And you, of course, never told him.' There was a curious twist to his lips. 'Otherwise he might have changed his mind about leaving you such a white elephant?'

'But the house isn't that bad,' she protested. 'With some money spent on it, it could be made into a really pleasant place to live in.' Then his insinuation made an impact. 'Just what are you implying, Mr Baird? That I was extra attentive to your great-uncle for my eventual personal gain?'

He just kept on looking at her, his expression unreadable.

'That's an insult! After all, haven't I turned down not just one, but *two* offers for the place?'

His dark, expression brows rose. 'It wouldn't be for mercenary reasons?'

The angry colour rose in her face. 'Are you implying that I'm just like the other women "in your experience"?' she quoted his words. 'That is, that I'm looking for the highest bidder?'

'Well, aren't you? What are you holding back for? For me to double my offer? Or maybe you intend to play me off against those property developers? Because you must know as well as I do that they won't take your first "no" for an answer. Nor, probably, your second.'

Furious now, Kirsten jumped up. 'Can't you get it into your head, Mr Baird, that I'm serious in my plans to restore Tall Trees?'

He was unmoved, rising to face her, his hard, handsome face firming around the stubborn, square jaw. 'No, I can't, Miss Ingram. No one in their right minds—certainly their right business minds—could look around this place as I've just done and see in it any possiblities whatsoever for restoration and renovation.'

'I'm not talking about *business,* Mr Baird,' she said almost desperately, 'but about the house I live in. Can't you understand—this is my *home*! I gave up the digs I had all those years ago when I came to work for Mr Hazelton. I can't return to my parents. Their house is too small for them to take me back, and, in any case, my sister is still living there with them, so there wouldn't be any room for me.'

'With the money I'm willing to pay for Tall Trees,' Scott countered, 'you'd be able to buy yourself a modern property, say a flat or a small house, and you'd have enough money left over to rehouse your parents too.'

'They don't *want* to be rehoused!' Kirsten exclaimed. 'They wouldn't thank me if I offered to. Nor do I want to move from here.'

For a long moment he studied her. His mouth was a tight line, his eyes as dark as the night sky. A feeling stirred inside her as she returned his look, her head high, but her heart was pounding like a jungle drum.

She thought, I'm fighting a battle all right, not just one, but two—my own feelings included. But she had the most awful premonition that all the weapons were on his side.

No, she corrected herself, that wasn't true. She had one weapon—potent and powerful and age-old, but she blushed at the thought of using it on this tough and cynical man. If at that moment, she reflected, he had been able to see into her mind, he would dismiss her contemptuously as one of those women he had known who 'gave away their sensuality' and never their hearts. My heart, she told her secret self—it's his any time he wants it. Then she realised with a profound shock just where her thoughts had been leading her, not only on to a very dangerous terrain, but to a very decided dead end.

His eyes narrowed, his gaze zipping assessingly up and down and all over her. Had he, she wondered with horror, guessed her thoughts, after all? Had something escaped through an unguarded look she hadn't even realised she had given?

He came nearer, his hand moving towards her. It closed over her upper arm and she shivered involuntarily, her eyes caught and held by his. She was mesmerised by him, a stranger who had walked into her life a little over an hour ago.

He had, for a few fleeting, but strangely exciting moments, held her in his arms. Those arms had offered her comfort, but they could, she was certain, offer a woman so very much more.

He released her, a faint smile curving over his well shaped mouth. 'We must keep in touch,' he said softly. 'I've given you my card. You know where to find me.'

'Why should I want to?' she queried. 'Find you, I mean?' She had intended the question to be an expression of the anger his whole uncooperative attitude had provoked within her, but it came out with an inflection that required a reply.

'Why, indeed?' he returned with a slow, mocking smile.

He left by the same french windows through which he had entered, striding away across the garden towards the gate which led to the orchard and his own land, which surrounded hers like a sea washing up against the shores of a lonely island, and slowly but relentlessly wearing it away.

CHAPTER TWO

ONE week later, the promising March sunshine vanished as if it never had been. Winter returned, and with it came unseasonable blizzards and snowdrifts that kept Kirsten prisoner in Tall Trees for five long days.

The telephone was cut off for two of them, leaving her more alone and isolated than ever before. Even Cherry Marston was unable to fight her way through the snowdrifts on her usual day.

Kirsten knew the telephone had been reconnected when it rang on the Saturday morning, just after breakfast. She ran to it eagerly, hoping it was Cherry saying the village was clear and she could get through.

'Miss Ingram?' the caller said. 'I'm wondering if you've been affected by the snowstorms in your part of the world. I've been trying to contact you for a couple of days. Are you all right?'

Kirsten could hardly believe that it was Scott Baird, concerned enough about her to be ringing to enquire. 'I'm fine, thank you,' she answered stiffly, doing her best to quell the unexpected spurt of pleasure the sound of his voice was causing inside her. 'The phone's been out of order, and I've been cut off from the village, but I had some spare tins of food, so I've managed. They say a thaw's on the way, so I should be fine now. Thank you for calling.'

It seemed he was not the kind of person to take hints. 'How's the fabric of the house standing up to the weather?'

'It's very cold and damp, unfortunately. I can't cope with lighting the fires in all the rooms, which Mr Hazelton used to have going in the grates. Cherry's husband from the village came to light them every day, but I can't afford to pay him now.'

She paused for a comment that never came.

'I've discovered that there's a lot of dampness in the downstairs rooms, as well as the upstairs. Especially the kitchen.' Again there was silence. 'I did tell you it needs a lot of money spent on it, Mr Baird.'

'And I told you, Miss Ingram, that I'd be willing to give you that money, in exchange for the house itself.'

Kirsten was silent, trying to sort throught her thoughts. Suddenly, the idea of being relieved of the worries which were mounting day by day was almost too inviting to resist. Then she remembered Mr Hazelton's wish that she should become owner of Tall Trees because she would take the greatest care of it. And an idea came out of the blue.

'If I thought you would let me stay here, Mr Baird, after the sale . . .' The rasp of his breathing sounded harsh in her ear. 'After the renovations,' she pressed on determinedly, 'I'd be glad to act as housekeeper, looking after it . . . Unpaid, of course . . .'

'No deal, Miss Ingram, sorry.' The words came over softly, the click of his receiver, although equally quiet, was dismayingly decisive.

Two days later the promised thaw arrived, bringing chaos with it. Water percolated through from the roof, through the loft, into the upstairs' rooms. The bedroom walls glistened with damp. Snow melted outside, creeping under the door into the kitchen, flowing in as fast as Kirsten was able to mop it up.

Cherry arrived at full speed, pushing up her sleeves and taking the soaking cloth from Kirsten's hands. The telephone rang and she dived for it, hoping against hope that it was Scott Baird again.

'Hi!' It was Peter Harvey, brother of her friend Marianne. For a year or two, between Robin's visits, he had been trying unsuccessfully to date Kirsten.

'Not now, Peter—I'm up to my ankles in water. No, wait!' It had just occurred to her that his would at least be a helping hand, especially as he was a junior architect with a firm in the town four miles away. 'Peter, I'm in terrible trouble and I need your help.'

'Ah!' Kirsten could almost see his grin. 'What kind of trouble? And what kind of help? If it's something your boyfriend Robin is responsible for——'

'Peter! Trust you to think of such a thing. Anyway, Robin's past history. He's not my——'

'He's not? You kidding, Kirsten? It's over, then?'

'It's over, Peter, but I'm not in the market for a substitute for him, only friendship, which you already give me. It's the house—it's leaking like a sieve from top to bottom. Cherry's here, but all she can do is mop up. I'm desperate for a strong man about the place to plug the holes and do repairs. Please, Peter?'

'When you put it like that, Kirsten . . . Give me ten minutes.'

He made it in five, swinging his ancient sports car in a crackling semicircle in the gravel. He sprinted up the stone steps and leaned on the bell until Kirsten ran to open it. 'Make way for the professional,' he ordered, striding past her. 'Where's the worst of the damage?'

'Upstairs.' She watched him take the stairs two at a time. 'And downstairs too. Everywhere, in fact,' she added miserably. 'There's hardly a room that's escaped.'

She followed him up, his tuts growing louder as the moments passed. 'How long,' he asked seriously, 'do you intend staying on in this place?'

They were downstairs now. Cherry was still busy mopping up. 'Indefinitely. It's the only home I've got,' said Kirsten.

'Have you also got a small fortune tucked away so you can pay for renovation? No, that's too mild a word. Rebuilding's more suitable in the circum-stances.'

'Not a penny.' Kirsten looked up at him—he was tall and curly-haired and well built—and saw the concern in his eyes. 'I've had an offer for the place, though.'

'So, what are you waiting for?'

'I told you, I just don't want to leave Tall Trees. And Mr Hazelton——'

'Was a sensible man. If he'd seen the house as it is today, the mess it's in——'

'It's no use trying to persuade me, Peter. I'm going to try and raise the money for restoration.' Her voice rang with a confidence she was beginning to feel. 'There must be something Mr Hazelton left here that I can sell.'

They had wandered into the library and Kirsten looked round anxiously in case the dampness had taken hold in there, threatening its contents. To her relief, there was no sign that it had.

She stared at the shelves, stacked with volumes, and with a flash of excitement she exclaimed, 'There's the answer!'

Peter's eyes followed Kirsten's. 'You'd sell those? Hey, that would be sacrilege! Some of those might be first editions.' He slid out a well worn leather-bound volume, then another. 'Two here, for a start. They're valuable, Kirsten.'

'They are?' She closed her ears to the memory of Mr Hazelton saying, 'I'd like the library to remain intact, my dear. Some of the books have great value, and members of my family know this. Like the house, I should wish that they at least would remain untouched, to be passed on to future generations of my brother's and sister's families.'

Kirsten had nodded, telling him, 'I'll do my very best, Mr Hazelton, to keep your library collection intact.'

The sigh of regret she gave came from the heart. 'Try to understand, Peter,' she pleaded. 'Although Mr Hazelton left me the house, only a small amount of money was put aside to help me maintain it. What he didn't know was how much it had deteriorated. I'm sure that, if he could see it as it is today, he'd tell me to do everything I could to save it, whatever the sacrifice.'

Peter came back that evening. They were walking in the rose garden which, for much of the year, acted as a colourful and scented backdrop to the paved terrace.

Beyond this there was an extensive area of lawn, bordered by flowering shrubs. Watching the birds swooping from branch to branch, Kirsten found herself thinking yet again about the man who owned the land beyond the gardens. Since the last time she had spoken to him, he had scarcely been out of her mind.

She couldn't forget his eyes, the shape of his face, the way it had felt to be comforted by those strong arms. There was a movement beyond the shrubs that formed a barrier between the gardens and the orchard. It couldn't be, she thought, she was imagining it. But it was, and it was as if she had conjured him up with her thoughts!

'Don't look now,' said Peter out of the corner of his mouth, then with a strange kind of deliberation lifted his arm and placed it across her shoulders, 'but there's an intruder walking around among those trees at the end of your garden.'

'He's not an intruder, Peter,' she answered under her breath, 'that's the new owner of Mr Hazelton's estate.'

'You kidding?' he asked.

'It's the truth.' She stared at the moving figure and felt oddly guilty. It was the way he was looking at them, particularly herself, as if she had committed adultery without even being married.

Was he remembering, she wondered, the way she had cried when Robin had given her the brush-off? Judging by the flash of contempt in his eyes as he directed a peremptory nod in their direction, Kirsten was sure he was thinking that not only had her broken heart mended with surprising speed, but that she was fickle and shallow in her personal relationships.

Was he thinking, she wondered, that she had turned on those tears when Robin had ditched her, just to get his, Scott Baird's, sympathy? Worse, had he scornfully decided that she was in the market for any man who happened to be available and willing?

He made as if to approach, but at that moment Peter pulled her closer. The action seemed to make Scott Baird change his mind, since he turned and disappeared through a gate into a field belonging to Hazel Farm, which he had also inherited from his great-uncle.

'Whew!' exclaimed Peter, pretending to mop his brow. 'That man was shooting out electrical charges like an overhead power line!'

For some reason, Kirsten found herself shivering. She looked at Peter. 'You felt it too, did you?'

'It's a wonder,' he commented, 'we didn't both go up in flames! Hey,' he stared down at her, a small grin on his face, 'did he think I was trespassing where you were concerned? I mean, he didn't inherit *you* along with the Hazelton estate?'

Kirsten laughed at the idea. 'You mean, does he fancy me?' She smiled broadly at the sheer absurdity of the thought. But, ridiculous though the idea was, it made her tingle to the ends of her toes. 'Now it's you who's got to be kidding,' she commented firmly, as much to convince herself as well as Peter. 'To a man like that, I'm like a tadpole in an enormous ocean of available females!'

The only person Kirsten could think of to give her advice about the sale of Mr Hazelton's books was Mr Phipps. So, the next day, she rang him.

'Sell the contents of Mr Hazelton's library, Miss Ingram?' he exclaimed, his dismay coming at her over the telephone line.

'The house is falling apart, Mr Phipps,' she answered, starting to despair. 'What am I going to use for money to save the place? The cash Mr Hazelton left me was for maintenance, not repair.'

He tutted, plainly worried on her behalf.

'My savings are going down so fast, Mr Phipps,' she went on, 'I'll have to go round with a begging bowl soon just to buy the neccessities of life, let alone get someone to plug the leaks where the rain comes in, install better ventilation to cure the damp . . .'

Tears had formed in her eyes as the realisation dawned of how impossible the whole situation was.

Mr Phipps' grunt became a long-suffering sigh. 'I'll get in touch with some contacts of mine who might be interested in buying the books.' He tutted again. 'It seems such a pity to have to let those first editions go, since I know how Lennard prized them. Nevertheless, I do appreciate your difficulties, Miss Ingram, and I'll do my best on your behalf.'

Her exclamation of gratitude plainly embarrassed him, since his grunts changed their pitch to a slightly more agreeable sound.

Two mornings later, Kirsten rang Peter at work. At once she wished she had not, since he dampened her spirits with a few destructive but painfully sensible words. 'Even if you were to sell the books at top price,' he cautioned, 'it wouldn't give you the money you need, not by a long way.'

Her fingers gripped the receiver. 'Peter, what shall I do? I'm desperate! Plus I've had a headache for two days.' And a throat like sandpaper, she thought, but did not say.

'If you really want my opinion, Kirsten,' he returned with painful frankness, 'I suggest you think again about that offer you've had. If you sell the place——'

'I know all the arguments,' Kirsten broke in, 'but Tall Trees in mine. It remains mine. It was left to me in good faith to look after, so I intend to do just that. I'll fight with everything I've got to keep it.'

'That's OK,' soothed Peter. 'Don't jump down my throat—I was only trying to help. Any chance of seeing you this evening?'

'You wouldn't enjoy it,' Kirsten answered, nursing her tender neck glands. 'I've got a cold coming, I'm sure. Think I'll have an early night.'

'OK,' he repeated cheerfully. 'Maybe tomorrow?'

'Maybe,' she responded dully. 'Who knows?'

It was after lunch that a ring at the door dragged her out of the armchair she had sunk into, a scarf looped for comfort around her aching throat.

A man stood there expectantly, a scholarly stoop to his shoulders. He held out his card. 'Oliver Stewartson,' it announced, 'Antiquarian Bookseller.' It carried a London address. His slightly battered estate car stood in the driveway. Antiquarian too, Kirsten thought, hiding a wry smile.

Her eyes had brightened considerably, along with her spirits. 'You've come to look at Mr Hazelton's library?'

The man nodded. 'I'm an old acquaintance of Mr

Phipps. He told me that there were some volumes that might be of interest to me.'

Kirsten pulled the door wide, anxious for him to enter, even more anxious for him to be impressed with the library's worth. 'First editions too, Mr Stewartson.' Proudly she showed him into the long bright room. 'In fact, all the books are old. I—er— didn't really want to part with them, but . . .'

Oliver Stewartson was not listening. 'Hm,' he remarked, eyeing the shelves with the faint scepticism of one who had heard it all before. Half an hour later he muttered 'Hm' again, but it was more of a sigh. Kirsten almost forgot to breathe. Was he truly disappointed, she wondered, or was he playing a professional game of downgrading the value to try to obtain a sale at a lower price?

'Some of the books are interesting,' he commented at last, 'some of them more than that. But——'

Which was the word Kirsten had been dreading. She asked the crucial question. 'What are they worth, Mr Stewartson?' The words almost caught in her painful throat.

He shook his head, putting away his notebook and pen. 'I'll make a considered valuation and let you know. Not a fortune, Miss Ingram,' he added at the door, 'not a fortune.' His smile seemed to crack his dry face and wrinkle his pointed nose. 'I'll contact you in a few days.' He nodded and was gone.

At the antique library table, Kirsten sank into the chair and put her head on her folded arms. A face drifted across the dark backdrop of her closed eyes; thick hair tossed by the wind, brown eyes watchful and more than a little derisive as they homed in across the expanse of the garden, sending their message of scorn for a woman whose motto was, in his unalterable opinion, 'off with the old love, on with the new'.

Firmly, she told herself she must face the inevitable. She liked the man, more than liked him. Those moments in his arms had done more to her than two whole years of Robin's friendship and kisses had ever done.

But where, she mused, did that get her? It simply multiplied her troubles. Becoming involved with Scott Baird on a business footing was one thing, but mixing that business with the hot potato of emotion was quite another.

All the same, she reflected, staring at the telephone, he was her only lifeline to achieving her object, that of saving Tall Trees from extinction. Then she remembered that when she had challenged him as to what he would do with the house if she ever decided to accept his offer to buy, his answer had been unequivocal—demolition.

The thought of Tall Trees becoming a mere pile of rubble made her shudder. No—she rested her aching head again—she couldn't go across to that telephone and repeat to him her request for help.

A few minutes later the ring of the phone shattered the peace of the library. Hand shaking, she answered. 'Kirsten Ingram here.' Would Scott Baird be at the other end? She told herself she was stupid even to think of it.

'This is Constance Cole, Mr Baird's secretary, Miss Ingram,' the voice announced. 'Mr Baird would like to see you, if that's at all possible?' She paused, plainly waiting for confirmation.

'Oh—er—yes. Yes, of course,' Kirsten answered, still not believing her luck. He had changed his mind and was going to help her! He *was* calling from his place of work, she reminded herself, which was a bank, wasn't it?

'Would tomorrow be convenient?' the secretary hustled. 'Mid-morning?' She named a time and rang off.

What did it matter now, Kirsten thought, her spirits rocketing, that her head still ached and her throat felt as if she had swallowed gravel? Scott Baird was going to help her after all!

Constance Cole was as elegant and efficient as her voice had implied. 'You look a little pale, Miss Ingram, if you'll forgive me for saying so. Can I get you something? Coffee, perhaps? Mr Baird is not quite ready for you.'

'Coffee would be fine,' Kirsten answered, touching her throat, around which she had arranged a pink silk scarf to set off the pearl grey of her suit; and to soothe away the continuing soreness.

As she drank, she hoped that her make-up, which she had applied more liberally than usual to disguise her shadowed eyes, had not been overdone. She'd hate to give Scott Baird the impression, she thought sarcastically, that, having recovered from Robin at lightning speed, as he plainly believed, she had pushed even Peter aside and was after bigger fish—no less a person than Scott himself!

Those shrewd brown eyes which met her at the door, and for which she had begun to look in every passing face, saw something in her appearance, she sensed, to firm his mouth into a set line. Now what have I done? she wondered.

A few moments later, facing him across his huge desk, she knew what it was. 'Is your boyfriend hanging around downstairs waiting for you?'

Kirsten frowned, caught off guard by a question that sounded like an accusation. 'Boyfriend?' she queried, genuinely puzzled. 'There's no one in my life now who goes by that description, as I'm sure you know. So no, Mr Baird, there's no one waiting for me.' He still did not seem convinced, so she went on, 'You know about Robin and me. You were there when he called from Holland to end our——'

'I'm talking about his successor,' Scott Baird cut in grimly.

'You're implying that Peter's taken his place?' Kirsten shook her head. 'When you saw us the other evening, he'd come to——'

'Don't go into details,' he interrupted forcefully. 'It's your business how quickly you're able to recover from a broken relationship—broken "heart", I believe the romantics call it, don't they?—and take on another.' His tone was cynical. 'A couple of weeks ago, when you cried all over me after your boyfriend ditched you, I was touched by your apparent distress. But it seems I was wasting my sympathy.'

'Were you?' she answered dully, hating his abrasiveness and longing instead for his sympathy.

When, she fretted, would he give her the good news? Was he staying silent to keep her guessing, as a way of punishing her, as he thought, for her fickleness where her men friends were concerned?

He leaned back in his swivel chair, hands resting on the arms, eyes hooded and watchful. 'You look pale,' was his summing up, echoing his secretary's opinion.

So much, Kirsten thought, for the time she had spent highlighting her eyes, disguising with subtle colour tones the visible evidence of the way she felt.

'Too many late nights,' she flipped back, uncaring that she might be confirming in his mind that Peter had not only taken Robin's place in her life, but in her bed too.

'Try saying "no" a bit more often, Miss Ingram,' Scott drawled sarcastically, leaning forward, hands clasped on his desk. 'It's a wonderful restorative of flagging energies. And a rest now and then does everyone good.'

She wanted to throw her bag at him, but instead she gripped it harder on her lap. 'Is this why you brought me here, Mr Baird?' she questioned grittily. 'To cross-examine me about my private affairs?'

'No.' He turned crisp and businesslike, drawing a sheet

of paper towards him, his eyes skimming its contents. 'I understand from Mr Phipps that you're in a bad way financially.'

Mr Phipps, Kirsten thought, had no right to discuss her troubles with this man. But maybe the solicitor had done his best for her?

'If you're talking about a loan for renovating Tall Trees,' she took him up eagerly, 'it's very good of you to——'

'Who said anything about a loan?'

'N-no loan?'

'No loan.' He leaned back, his eyes reflectively on her. 'You know very well that my mind is made up on that matter. I told you my opinion of the state of your residence.'

'That it should be bulldozed to the ground,' she said bitterly, getting to her feet. 'Thank you for the coffee.'

Scott was round the desk and at the door before she could open it. Far from being pale now, her cheeks were burning. 'We're both wasting our time. And yours is so very much more valuable—and expensive—than mine, Mr Baird, isn't it?'

His grip bruised her arms. She jerked away, but he took her shoulder and led her back to the chair. 'There are other ways of helping you, moneywise. Sit down, Miss Ingram. If you stay put long enough,' a satirical smile pulled at his mouth, 'you might just hear something to your advantage.'

'Nothing,' she answered vehemently, 'matters as much to me as that loan I'm not allowed to have.'

He ignored the statement, running a finger along a line of type in Mr Phipp's letter. 'Your solicitor tells me you are doing two jobs of work of a family nature, completely without remuneration. Typing my great-uncle's memoirs——'

'That was one of the conditions of my inheriting the house. I'm only too happy to do it.'

'A labour of love?' One eyebrow lifted itself, two deep brown cynical eyes mocked.

'Why shouldn't it be?' she flared, knowing exactly what he was thinking. 'Your great-uncle was a kindly, thoughtful person, a man of whom one could—and I did—become very fond. And if you dare to imply again that I stayed with him because I knew what would eventually come my way——'

Both eyebrows arched themselves in unison. 'What was coming your way?' He asked the question as if he genuinely wanted to know.

'Tall Trees. What else?'

He thought for a moment, then from across the desk gave her a dark-brown look that did something strange to her heartbeats.

'I understand,' he said, 'that my great-uncle left you only sufficient money for the maintenance of the property. In other words, nothing with which to feed and clothe yourself while you were working on his memoirs.'

Kirsten lifted her shoulders. 'I wish Mr Phipps hadn't told you so much about my affairs.'

'Don't worry.' Scott leaned back, the whole solid bulk of him. 'He didn't do it without some reservations, or without pressure on my part. In fact, he only told me after I'd said I might be able to help you with your monetary problems.'

'There's only one problem that really worries me, Mr Baird,' she replied doggedly, 'and you know what that is.'

He went on as if she had not spoken. 'There is one job you're doing that's entirely on my behalf.'

'Looking after the Hazelton—sorry, the Baird—estate? It was part of my work with your great-uncle. It didn't go away when he—went away. So I just carried on doing it.'

'Again, without remuneration.'

That was something which she couldn't deny. 'I've been living on what I've managed to save over the years.'

'Which is dwindling.'

Mr Phipps again! she thought. Her cheeks felt as if they were on fire. She was beginning to wonder if she had a temperature. The painkilling tablets she had taken before leaving home were starting to wear off and she knew she had to get back to home ground before that ground came up and hit her.

'Mr Baird,' she said faintly, 'I'm sorry, but I have to go.' She made to stand, but his hand came out, its movement urging her down again.

'I insist,' he said, 'on paying you a salary for this work you're doing for me. What's more,' he got up and came round the desk again, standing over her, 'I intend to recompense you for the money you've had to draw out of those savings of yours to do this work for me.'

Kirsten was about to protest when he lifted his hand.

'Postage, for instance,' he went on, 'phone bills, not to mention the cost of your time. And the sheer ability inside here,' his hand rested on the top of her head, pressing it gently back so that he could look into her eyes, 'to cope with the job single-handed.'

She moistened her cracked lips. 'There's absolutely no need——'

Scott was frowning. 'Your head's on fire! What's wrong, Kirsten?'

Her heart flipped over at his use of her name, at the unexpected concern in his eyes. 'Hangover,' she improvised. 'Late nights—I told you.'

The concern was wiped away, cynicism taking its place. 'I've booked a table for two at——'

'No!' The word escaped her lips without warning. 'Thank you,' she added more quietly. Her throat was so painful, she felt sure she would hardly be able to swallow liquid, let alone portions of exotic food at some top-class restaurant. The cough she had been suppressing with the help of the pain-killers surfaced, and it shook her chest and back.

'Sorry.' She gazed weakly up at him. 'Next time,' she tried to joke, 'I really will have to reduce my alcohol intake!' Then she shivered, despite the reasonably mild early April day.

This time, Scott let her make it to the door.

'Thanks for the thought,' she said, turning. 'Sorry to mess up your lunch plans. And I'm grateful for your offer of a salary for looking after your land around Tall Trees. But don't give it another thought. After all, if you did pay me, I'd have you as my employer, wouldn't I? And that, Mr Baird, would be the very last thing I'd want to happen!'

'Did you get the loan you were after?' Peter had called in to hear the good news Kirsten had been so certain she would bring back from London.

One look at her face told him the answer. It also told him that she was far from well. And, if he needed confirmation of this, a bout of coughing shook her.

The spring evening was cool, but the need for economy had forced her to switch off the already inadequate central-heating system.

'He had no intention of lending me any money, Peter,' Kirsten said wearily from the depths of an armchair. 'He invited me to see him to tell me he thought it was time he paid me some money for managing the Baird estate.'

'Well?' He looked incredulous. 'You don't mean you turned down his offer?' As she nodded, he exploded, 'Kirsten, you're mad! You tell me you've hardly any savings left, yet when someone does the right thing by you and says he'll pay you for work done, you stick your nose in the air and——'

'I don't want Scott Baird as my employer!' she retorted. 'It's bad enough being the owner of a house in the middle of land that belongs to him, without having to play the sycophant to his big boss act.' Peter shook his head in disbelief. 'He was going to take me to lunch,' she added tiredly.

'Was going to? You mean, you even turned that down?'

'I just didn't feel hungry,' she answered in a small voice. 'And I couldn't have managed the small talk, either. Know what? He offered to send me all the way home in a taxi. At his expense.'

'Offered? You mean, you said "no" to that, too?' She nodded. 'Have you gone crazy? Has the London air gone to your head or something?'

Kirsten said hoarsely, 'I think I've got a temperature.'

Peter felt her forehead. 'You're burning hot.'

'That's what Mr Baird said. I told him I had a hangover.'

'And he believed you?'

Kirsten nodded, then made a face, because it hurt to move her head. 'Peter,' she said faintly, 'mind if I go to bed?'

'I'd mind if you didn't.' He went towards the telephone. 'What's your doctor's number?'

'I'm not telling you—I don't want a doctor. You can go now. Thanks for coming.'

'Think I'd leave you in this state? I'm staying until you're all tucked up.' He patted the top of her head, but stopped when she winced. 'Then I'll bring you a nice cup of hot milk. Agreed?'

'Peter,' she sighed, 'you're a real friend.'

'I'd like to be more.'

She made a face at his statement that turned into an

appeal, and mouthed the words, 'No, sorry.'

Fifteen minutes later, he carried the steaming mug up the winding staircase and looked in every room until he found Kirsten's. 'It's absolutely crazy,' he commented, 'one person living alone in a place this size. Twenty rooms, you said? The whole building ought to be——'

'Knocked down, demolished. I know, I've had that opinion thrown at me already, by Scott Baird. He said if he bought Tall Trees from me, that's what he'd do to it.'

'So you said "no".'

'It's a habit of mine.' She stretched out eager hands for the milk, and Peter shook out a couple of tablets. 'Found them in the medicine cabinet. Help you through the night.' Kirsten swallowed them. 'Sure you wouldn't like me to stay, Kirsten? Just say the word. I saw a room back there with the bed already made up.'

'Thanks, Peter, but no.' She took a drink of milk and he sat on the side of the bed. 'Peter, you're a pet for this.'

'That's OK. I'm ingratiating myself with you to take the place of your ex-boyfriend.'

'No chance. I'm having a rest from men.' The face of one particular man flashed in front of her aching eyes. It did nothing to soothe them, instead, it dazzled and tormented and derided. If, she thought, I wanted any man's arms around me, it wouldn't be Peter's. But, she reasoned, Scott's arms wouldn't be good for me, either. They might have calmed her once but, even feeling as she did, she knew they would have a very different effect on her now.

Peter accepted the empty mug, then took her hand. 'Look, I'll stay. I'll call my parents and tell them I won't be home tonight.'

There was a sound at the bedroom door. Startled, she stared past Peter. She saw the bulk of a man standing there and her heart almost stopped.

'Miss Ingram?'

Of all people, of all men, she thought, Scott Baird had to appear at that moment! Unannounced, uninvited, he had walked himself into her house and all the way up the stairs.

CHAPTER THREE

'I CALLED out,' said Scott, 'but no one answered.' His eyes sliced from Kirsten to her companion. *Too wrapped up in each other,* they derided, their silent message louder than any spoken words.

Peter stood up, his eyes as wide as Kirsten's. Did you know he was coming? he was asking her silently. Of course I didn't, her glance rebuked him.

'I'm off,' said Peter in a let's-get-out-of-here voice. 'I'll give you a call in the morning, Kirsten.' He squeezed her hand, and she sensed he was trying to give her courage. He made a sooner-you-than-me face and paused at the door, waiting for Scott Baird to allow him through.

'Don't let me break up the party,' drawled Scott, lifting himself languidly from the doorframe. His eyes flicked over Kirsten like a whip. Only then did she remember that, in her hurry to get into bed, she had pulled on the first nightgown that had come to hand, a filmy pink affair that Peter's sister Marianne had given her one birthday and which she had never worn before. No doubt, Kirsten thought, Scott Baird assumed she had put it on for Peter's benefit.

Peter looked back at her over his shoulder and gave a helpless shrug, then his footsteps descended the stairs in record time.

'I can understand your coming to look over your estate,' Kirsten said, with as much dignity as the circumstances allowed, and through a throat which made her voice sound strangled, 'but what escapes me is how you managed to get into my house.'

'You'd omitted to lock the door,' Scott answered crushingly. 'Next time your boyfriend comes to stay the night, a little more discretion might pay off.'

She opened her mouth to deny his assertion, when a bout of coughing overtook her. Crossing her arms weakly over her chest, she turned her face away, finding the pillow.

'As I thought.' The angry words were spoken under his breath. 'Hangover be damned! You're ill.'

'No, I'm not,' she began to protest feebly, when the pain-killers began to work and her body started to relax. 'Just tired,' she added, 'that's all.'

'Another lie,' murmured Scott, putting a hand on her forehead. 'Late nights, she said, too much alcohol! Did my great-uncle know he employed, and thought so much of, an expert teller of untruths? And that's putting it politely.'

'When you go,' she murmured, closing her eyes just before sleep had its way, 'will you please lock the front door?' Which, if she hadn't been so feverish and lightheaded, she would have realised was an impossible feat for any departing visitor to have accomplished.

'And,' she added, not even knowing if he was still there, 'even if Peter had been intending to stay the night, which he wasn't, it would only have been to look after me.'

But, since there was not even a movement in response, Kirsten assumed that Scott Baird had gone.

In the night a spasm of coughing woke her. She became hazily aware of that supportive arm again, and a glass of water being pressed to her lips.

The room was in almost total darkness and, in her dazed state, she reasoned that Peter must have returned. Then she sank back into a troubled sleep.

When she re-surfaced, she felt moist and shivery. Some-one's hands were sponging and drying her and tugging at her nightdress. Realising from the depths of the fever that gripped her that resisting was stupid when someone was doing their best to help, she co-operated.

A cool cotton garment was pulled over her head, and she lifted her body to make it easier for whoever it was to slide a hand under her and help her into the fresh nightdress.

When strong fingers eased the neckline together over her breasts, tying the bow, she delighted in their magic, cooling touch. Her eyes fluttered open in surprise, and she saw the outline of the man leaning over her.

For one crazy moment she thought it might be Scott, but, knowing that he had gone home hours ago, she told herself she was hallucinating. Was it Robin come back to her, deciding he liked her better, after all, than the other girl he had deserted her for?

Common sense brought her back to full consciousness and she stared with dulled but anxious eyes at the broad shoulders of the man who was now sitting on the side of her bed, his hand holding hers.

'Scott?' Her voice wavered weakly, the soreness in her throat still persisting. 'Why are you here? You went home——'

'I stayed,' was his succinct answer. 'Try to get some more sleep.'

His free hand reached over and stroked her hair, its back running down her burning cheek. She felt an over-powering urge to seize it and put it to her lips. What was happening to her? she wondered, her mind feverishly working at the problem, trying to analyse her reactions to this man who had touched her so intimately, yet with whom she quarrelled almost every time they met.

She looked around the room and made out a garden

lounger a couple of paces from her bed. 'You've been sleeping in here, on that?'

'Why not? I found a blanket.'

'It was probably damp,' she told him weakly. 'You should have aired it first. Everything in this house is damp until it's dried out.'

Scott nodded like a parent placating a fractious child. 'Now sleep some more.'

She shook her head. Remembering the prevailing dampness had reminded her that he could have made things better at Tall Trees if only he had agreed to help.

'There was no need,' she returned petulantly and with an ingratitude for his thoughtfulness that she regretted, but could not, in her present state, control, 'for you to have spent the night here just so you could play the nursemaid and salve your conscience about not giving me a loan. I'm not so ill I can't——'

'Will you be quiet?' The words came through clenched teeth. 'You're ill enough to have to accept whatever help's offered, whoever it might come from. Being involved with the Hazelton-Baird family affairs as you are, I feel responsible for your welfare.'

'Then,' she took him up, despite the fact that she felt so weak it tired her to talk, 'why haven't you felt *responsible* enough for me to give me the means to improve the house I live in . . .' The cough began again; by the end of it, she found his arms were round her and her cheek resting against his chest.

In the subdued light of the bedside lamp he looked dark and exciting, the sight of his unshaven state doing things to her feminine reflexes that shook her, despite the fact that her temperature was almost certainly way above normal.

She wanted them to stay as they were, their arms entwined, their bodies pressed close. She wanted him to lie beside her, so that she could cling to him for warmth and consolation. She found herself craving for his energy and vitality, wanting it to pass into her body and restore her to mobility and fitness. And, afterwards, for his masculine power and vigour—*and desire*—to reach out to her and draw her into him, making them as one.

She rubbed her face against him, inhaling his scent through the thin layer of his shirt. The fever was burning down her barriers, letting all her longings out of prison.

Gently, Scott lowered her to the pillows, resting his hand on her forehead.

'Have you singed your fingers?' she asked, attempting a wavering joke.

His smile in return was taut. 'I'm singeing more than that, believe me. And what's more,' he whispered, his lips a breath's caress from hers, 'you're doing your darnedest to help me go up in flames.'

'If I am, I'm sorry, but it's——' It's you, she had been going to say, you do something to the woman in me, even feeling as I do . . .

'Oh, don't apologise,' he returned drily. 'The pleasure's all mine.'

He started to move away, but she grabbed his hand. 'Don't leave me, *please*!' Don't go away, come closer, was what she had really meant.

He interpreted her plea differently—which, she reflected later, was just as well in the circumstances. 'I'll be here, Kirsten, lying beside you on this,' indicating the lounger.

In the half-light, she noticed how tired he looked. It was as much as she could do to prevent her arms from reaching out in a gesture, she tried telling herself firmly, of comfort. But the femininity in her knew better.

Scott's shirt was open, hanging loosely, his trousers creased. His chest, she saw, was broad and tanned from his travels abroad, and bore a dark fuzz that had cushioned her cheek as she had rested against it.

So this, she thought, was the human side of the autocratic banker who, only a few hours before, had addressed her so formally, his manner dauntingly brisk and businesslike. It seemed he had a heart, after all, even though it beat to the tune of tinkling coins, telephone bells and tapping computer print-outs from all over the world.

When she awoke late that morning, he was missing. There were voices drifting to her ears, male and authoritative. One was Scott's; the other she recognised as that of Mr Burns, the local builder.

'It's in a bad state of repair,' Mr Burns was grumbling. 'I don't think old Mr Hazelton knew that parts of his house were nearly falling about his ears. Otherwise he wouldn't have left it to her, that he wouldn't. I don't wonder she's ill!'

'Hm, I suspected that living in these conditions,' Scott remarked grimly, 'might have brought about her illness.'

'You'd need the constitution of an ox,' Fred Burns commented sagely, 'even if you're as young as she is, to stay healthy in this damp, cold house. Mausoleum, I'd call it. If I had my way, I'd——'

Scott must have silenced him, since he grunted and said no more. They must have descended the stairs, because the next time Mr Burns spoke, Kirsten had to strain to hear. 'I'll do my sums and give you a quote for the job. Either way, it won't be cheap, it's in such a state. I don't know as how the lass could afford to pay for it, really.'

'I'll take care of that,' Scott said briskly. 'You'll get your money, Fred, one way or another.'

'Well,' Kirsten could almost hear Mr Burns shifting his cap and scratching his head, 'a lot depends on whether you want the place patched up, or half-rebuilt, or what.' They moved out of earshot.

Scott, she realised unbelievingly, was making some kind of effort to get the house put to rights, and her heart started doing a slow, celebratory dance. So what, she reasoned, if it were not a complete renovation? Just making it rainproof and dry would enable her to stay on there, even if she couldn't yet fulfil her—and Mr Hazelton's—dream.

Cooler now, she guessed the fever had left her. Feeling the need of a good wash, she made her way to the bathroom. Her legs felt as shaky as those of a day-old lamb, but she forced herself to carry out her toilet routine.

A tall, angry figure appeared outside the half-opened bathroom door, elbowing it wide. 'What the hell,' Scott exploded, 'do you think you're doing here?' His hands were on his hips, his legs belligerently apart.

He must have visited the village shop, Kirsten reckoned. Among other items it stocked everyday clothes, a selection of which he had obviously bought, since his legs and thighs filled a pair of tough blue denims that in no way echoed the impeccable cut of the dark city suit he had been wearing since his arrival the evening before. The navy short-sleeved shirt had probably been acquired from the same source, as it barely accommodated the breadth of his chest and shoulders, the three-buttoned opening plainly more comfortable unfastened. He exuded a hard masculinity that Kirsten had glimpsed in the semi-darkness of her bedroom in the early hours, and which now hit her squarely between the eyes.

The dark layer of hair on his arms underlined their hard-boned muscularity, the large stainless steel watch being more compatible, she reflected, with the side of him that she was seeing now than with his *alter ego,* a desk-bound London-based banker.

'I had to freshen up,' she told him, weakness overcoming the urge to snap at him that he was not her keeper. She started to creep through the doorway, but he scooped her up and carried her, protesting, back to bed. 'It's only a cold I've got,' she defied him, 'there's no need to make all this fuss. I'm getting up soon. I've got work to do——'

'Is that so?' He looked down into her face and sarcasm flecked his eyes. 'Work, is it, that's bothering you? Oh, no! The world wouldn't stop revolving if you didn't type another word of my great-uncle's memoirs.'

'Oh, but——'

'No "buts". And like hell you've only got a cold! It's on your chest. I think you're bronchitic.' He suspended her over the bed and she did not want him to put her down. 'And what's more, I'm calling the doctor.'

'No, thank you. That's what Peter wanted to do, but I wouldn't let him.'

'You,' he said, with some force, but with a lurking indulgence, 'are not bossing me about as you do your boyfriend.'

'Peter's not my——'

'OK, your lover, then.'

Despite her weakness, Kirsten tried to struggle. 'Lover he is not!' she answered, her voice rising despite the hoarseness. 'In your high and mighty world, can't a woman have a friend who's a man without her being emotionally involved with him?'

Scott spread his hands. 'You win. You aren't in a fit state for me to argue with you. The fact that he was here, in your bedroom, about to phone his family and tell them he was staying the night is, in my book, evidence enough of his closeness to you.'

Kirsten tried to wriggle out of his arms. 'I hate you,' she whispered, closing her eyes on tears of weakness and annoyance. 'I hate domineering men who use false arguments to prove their own *pig-headed* points!'

He still did not put her down, so she opened her eyes from which the tears immediately spilled over. There was a look in his eyes that would have turned her limbs to jelly if they had not already felt that way. His mouth was taking a relentless path towards hers and she found that she had no wish whatever to take avoiding action.

The kiss was sweet and intoxicating, bringing the heat back to her cheeks and a pounding to her pulses. It was not the burning warmth of fever. It arose from a fire that had been lit low down inside her and which was gaining a fierce, rising hold.

'Scott?' she whispered, hoping he could not decode the message in her eyes. He was only playing with her, she knew that, her nearness and the thinness of her covering having a perfectly natural effect on his male reflexes. Whereas she had never felt this way about a man in her life.

At last he lowered her, pulling up the cover. She lay staring at him, hoping he would put her wide, stunned gaze down to her illness.

In reality she was telling herself that this man, arrogant and dominating and, yes, *irritating* though he was, had found his way into her heart. If he ever asked for her love, it was there, in her hands, her arms and her eyes, for him—and him alone.

CHAPTER FOUR

'WHY are you still here?' Kirsten gladly swallowed the milky mid-morning coffee Scott had brought to her. Breakfast she had skipped, her appetite still non-existent.

The doctor had come and gone, his diagnosis confirming Scott's suspicions. The virus infection, he said, was playing havoc with her lungs. The tablets he was prescribing would help, but the illness would take its course and eventually clear itself.

Tender loving care, he had added, smiling brilliantly at Scott and then at Kirsten, as if he were there and then tying the bridal knot, would do the rest. Ever the romantic, Dr Woods, no longer young himself, had tended Lennard Hazelton to the end, often joining him for a drink and chat in the evenings after his work was done.

He had once met Scott—many years ago, he said—and he knew Kirsten well. Wasn't it time, his diagnostic eyes enquired, that Kirsten and Lennard's great-nephew together filled the vacancy in their respective lives for a permanent partner?

Scott's well defined eyebrows rose at Kirsten's question. 'I chose to stay. I could say it was—er—out of a sense of duty?'

Her heart wilted. If she had expected a more compelling reply, then she was the fool, wasn't she? 'Duty?' she took him up. 'You aren't under any obligation to me.'

'To my late relative, Lennard Hazelton. I couldn't go away, could I, leaving his pet lamb ill and neglected in her hour of need?'

Kirsten frowned up at him, suspecting laughter at her expense. She found it in his quirking lips. 'You can go,' she returned irritably. 'As far as I'm concerned, you've cleared your conscience of any guilt by staying with me overnight. Thank you for that.' She turned her face to the pillow. 'Cherry Marston will come for an hour or two and look after me.'

There was a short silence, during which Kirsten willed herself not to look at him, certain he was looking at her.

'Your boyfriend phoned.'

Her head swung round. 'Peter?' There, she thought, angry with herself, I've fallen into his trap. What use now denying that Peter's my boyfriend?

His hard smile told her he was pleased he had got the truth out of her at last. 'Yes—Peter. I told him I'd stayed with you through the night. I said it would be some days before you were in a fit state to entertain him again.'

His insinuating use of the word 'entertain' made her grind her teeth. 'But you're leaving soon. You could at least have asked him to come for an hour or two to keep me company.'

'Who said I'm leaving?'

'Well, aren't you?'

Scott side-stepped the question. 'What would you do if I refused to go?' He was bending over her now, his tooth-paste-clean breath fanning her face. 'Throw me out bodily?' He opened his arms, his rolled-up shirtsleeves revealing tanned, sinewy flesh. 'Come on,' his voice held a dare, 'see how far you get.'

He had set her heart racing again, and her washed-out cheeks were growing warm. She lifted her arm to push him away and made unintentional contact with his jaw. It was freshly shaved and the scent of his lotion was a balm to her illness-jaded sense of smell. He caught her hand and put it to his cheek, pulling her palm across his mouth and moving his lips over it until they reached the pulse point on her wrist. His eyes watched her all the time he made gentle, if unmistakable, love.

'Why,' she whispered huskily, 'are you doing this?' It was, she knew deep down, a little like asking a dragonfly why its wings shimmered and danced so beautifully. She shouldn't be questioning why this man was being so charming and seductive. Feeling as she did about him, she should be accepting his amorousness with open arms. *Then using it to coax him into giving her the financial help she really wanted from him . . .*

The fact that the thought should even occur to her of indulging in such deception brought on a fit of coughing. Those strong arms came out again, and this time she went into them gladly.

When it was over, she leant against his shoulder. 'You didn't answer my question,' she whispered, rubbing her face against his shirt and breathing in the shower-fresh scent of him.

'I might ask the same question of you,' countered Scott, bunching a fist under her chin and looking into her eyes. 'Why are you responding to me so lovingly? Or are you, in your weakened state, fantasising that I'm your ex-boyfriend?'

Am I, Kirsten wondered, dismayed, showing my feelings that clearly? She had to put him off the scent! 'No,' she answered crisply, 'just using my female attractions to try to persuade you to lend me that money.'

All the tenderness was wiped away, as she had known it would be. But she had had to put up a smokescreen to hide her feelings for him! She had to keep to herself how his presence aroused her, even from the torpor imposed by her illness; how the broad, hard sight of him excited in her sensations no man had ever aroused before.

But, in pretending to be manipulating him for her own

ends, she had paid the price of losing his tender tolerance.
His brown eyes glittered and he withdrew from all contact.
Walking to the window, he stared across the gardens to his
land.

Despite the aura of approachability the leisure garments
from the village store had woven around him, his personality was back in his banker skin, the human side of him
wiped clean away. His voice was aloof and brisk.

'There are one or two things I want to say to you,' he
said distantly. 'Are you feeling well enough to listen?'

'It depends on whether it's good news or bad,' Kirsten
prevaricated. Already her heart's beats were speeding up,
anticipating the announcement that, after careful reflection on the entire matter of the house and its adjacent
gardens, the cash advance she was after was hers . . .

Scott half turned and raised a quizzical eyebrow, then
spoke to the blossoms coming into flower in the bright
spring morning. 'I'll strike a bargain with you.' He
paused, as if trying to find the appropriate words. Her
heart broke into that dance again. The good news she had
been waiting for was coming now . . .

'I'll fund a repair job on this house if, in return, you'll
allow me to take over two or three rooms as a country
retreat.'

He waited for her answer, but her heart's dance was
slowing to a ragged stop. These were not the words she
had been so sure were coming her way at last.

'This morning,' he went on, seemingly unaware of her
deep disappointment, 'I called in a builder to look round
the place.'

'Mr Burns from the village,' she supplied unexcitedly. 'I
heard his voice.'

'He's giving me a quote for the job. I shall, of course,
show it to you as the owner before giving an answer.
Among other things,' he went on, 'I want the place made

watertight, damp-free and generally brought up to a standard where it's possible to live in it without contracting pneumonia. Or,' he moved to stand at the foot of her bed, 'its first cousin, bronchitis.'

'So,' she let out a long, sad sigh, 'no loan, Scott?' She still could not relinquish her dearest dream about complete renovation and conversion.

'No, no loan!' he snapped, on the verge of anger. 'I'm making a bona fide offer, Kirsten. I foot the bill for making this place truly habitable. You let me occupy some rooms in exchange. And I don't mean rent-free.'

She frowned. No cash to be handed over, but practical help offered none the less. 'You'd want to live here?'

Scott Baird, she thought, appearing without warning around any corner, bumping into him at any time of day—or night? It would, the pragmatic side of her said, take away the loneliness, fill the dark shadows with light. They would meet in the kitchen, in the hall, or on the way to bed.

'Weekends,' Scott was saying, 'occasional weekdays. The place is large enough, surely, for us not to fall over one another's feet? I wouldn't interfere with your——' his eyes moved over her bare arms as they lay on the cover '—affairs. Nor would I expect you to interfere with mine.'

Scott's affairs. Would she have to watch his women come and go? *And sometimes not go, but stay—and stay?*

'Well,' he prompted, 'what do you say?'

What would *he* say, she wondered, if she told him that, before giving him an answer, she would need to consult her feelings, her emotions—*her heart?* Was she strong enough to batten down her jealousy as each one of his sleeping partners came, stayed their allotted time, and went?

Just imagining his woman-type, slinky and glamorous, making her exotic way into his private—very private—

accommodation, made her hands clench and her toes curl.

'I don't know.'

'What else do you want?' he queried harshly. 'I'm willing to pay a rental that's higher than average. I'd furnish the rooms I occupied *and* the rest of the house, if that's what you want.'

Weakened though she was by the illness she had had, Kirsten's brain was not slow to grasp the possibilities for improvement which his suggestion and generous offer could bring about.

'The equipment in the kitchen is ancient,' she mentioned tentatively. 'And the curtains all round the house are so old, they're going into holes.'

He tugged a notebook and pencil from his rear trouser pocket. 'So make a list. Whatever renewals take your fancy . . .'

Accepting them, Kirsten noticed that Scott had made notes of Mr Burns' comments. 'Patched up or half-rebuilt? Damp course repair needed, roof tiles renewed, windows replaced, double glazing at extra cost . . .'

Kirsten managed a smile. 'You must want to share my house badly, to be prepared to spend so much money on it! Or is there a——' her smile almost faded '—a lady friend in your life you intend to install here? Because, if so, I'm afraid the answer's——'

'What kind of a fool do you take me for?' he barked. 'Do you honestly believe I'd bring a woman here, flaunt her under your nose——?'

Kirsten frowned, genuinely puzzled. 'Why would you want to keep your mistress a secret from me? Oh, now I understand. You think I'd tell the village, then the world? Leak it to the Press? Think of the headlines, "Top banker hides away his——" '

'It's quite obvious,' he broke in cuttingly, 'that you must be feeling better. Or is it your illness that's turned

you sour? Innuendo, sarcasm, threats . . .' He was beside
the bed, his hands curled as if he would dearly like to place
them around her throat. 'All I want is a country retreat,
away from the roar of London and its environs. From
constantly ringing telephones, from meetings, from
decision-making. And, most of all, away from people.
Now do you get my meaning?'

'A kind of sanctuary?' she suggested.

'If you like. For *myself,* understand?'

The thought came to her like a beautiful song—he
would be running for cover, for tranquillity to Tall Trees.
He woud be coming home—to *her*! What greater compliment, she wondered delightedly, could she ask for from
such a man.

'I'd expect,' he stated bluntly, 'to be left alone.'

It was, Kirsten thought, as if he'd sensed the trend of
her thoughts and decided to crush them underfoot.

'Don't worry,' she returned flatly, lying back against the
pillows, fatigue hitting her unexpectedly. 'I wouldn't
dream of trespassing on your privacy.'

'Nor I yours. So it's a deal?'

'It's a deal.' Why, she wondered tiredly, was there a
curious gleam in his eyes? 'And thank you.'

She held out her hand to seal the bargain. Instead of
shaking it, he took it, then, incredibly, lifted it, putting
first the wrist, then the palm to his lips. She could not keep
from her bright glance her quicksilver reaction to his
touch.

Scott's eyelids lowered and a very different expression
passed across his features. Almost as if something about
her was drawing him, his head slowly descended. By the
time his mouth touched hers, her lips were quivering with a
soft invitation. His kisses, as they traversed her mouth
from one corner to the order, were light but electrifying,
and essentially sexy.

When he lifted his head, Kirsten discovered to her dismay that her lips were pouting and parted and, as if they had acquired a will of their own, indisputably asking for more. Their glistening come-again plea was not granted, but the man who had resisted their sensual invitation seemed to know exactly what he was doing.

'Now,' those hard brown eyes held a glimmer of amusement—and something else Kirsten could not define, 'I must look after my future landlady's health. Where are those pills the doctor prescribed?' He shook two on to his palm, gave her some water and held her in a sitting position while she took them.

She shivered, although she was warm, and knew it was the rub of his bare arm around her back that had caused it. She looked up at him to thank him, but her glance caught sight of those lips that, only a few moments before, had brought hers to life.

It was an effort to tear her eyes away and, annoyed with herself, and with Scott for being so attractive, she snapped, 'There was no need to help me like that. I'm perfectly capable of sitting up without assistance!'

His raised eyebrows conveyed so much more than the reproach he could have levelled at her for her ingratitude. We know very well why you didn't actively dislodge my arm, don't we? they were saying.

It was no use, she told herself, she couldn't fight him in her weakened physical state. But had she really wanted to? Her secret answer to her own query forced her to question herself soberly as he lowered her gently back. Was she being stupid in agreeing to his proposition when it meant having the equivalent of a load of dynamite walking around her house? A constant danger to her peace of mind, seeing him at every turn of the corridor? Even just the knowledge that he was somewhere around, threatening at any unforeseen moment to stir up her emotions?

'Scott?' He was at the window, staring out. 'What made you change your mind about putting money into Tall Trees?' He swung round and she held up her hand. 'All right, I know it's not a loan.' His annoyance subsided. 'But the cash you say you're prepared to put into the place will be quite a large amount if you pay for all those things you've written in this notebook. Plus the refurnishing you promised to do. Added on to anything I might decide I want.' She indicated the notebook he had handed her. 'Which was very generous of you and very kind.'

He sauntered towards her, hands in pockets, his long limbs rippling with sinewy muscle. 'You ask me a question like that, when you're lying in bed laid low by the side-effects of living in a damp-ridden property that leaks like a fisherman's net whenever it rains or snows?'

'But,' she frowned, a little bewildered, 'you're under absolutely no obligation to me. There's no need at all for you to worry about me, either healthwise or financially. When I asked you for a loan, I meant it as such, not a gift. I'd have been prepared to pay it back in whatever instalments you dictated. It would have been on an entirely business footing.'

'Hard-headed businessman I may be, Kirsten,' he smiled down at her and her cheeks were flushed with a different kind of fever, 'but compassion I do have, when the circumstances call for it.'

He sat down, his taut thighs within reach of her fingers, which she had to force to stay still.

'If you could see yourself lying there,' he went on, 'pale and washed out, while your large eyes stare up at me like a helpless fawn's, you'd realise why I couldn't turn and walk away. Besides,' he took her hand and placed it on his thigh, holding it there firmly even when she tried to pull away, 'I'd had second, and third, thoughts about the place. Maybe I'd been a little too hard on it, condemning it in my mind to extinction. Maybe I began to think it had distinct possibilities in its very pleasant setting.'

The feel of his tough flesh under her fingertips was doing nothing to cool down the heat in her cheeks. If, she reflected, she knew—as she did—that at that moment she was looking anything but 'pale and washed out', then he must know it too. Had he even begun to wonder why?

'And,' she suggested, 'coming to live here weekends or whatever would give you a wonderful opportunity to keep an eye on your estate?'

'Not to mention,' a fist was pressed under her chin, 'keeping those same eyes on the young woman who's running it for me.'

'You mean,' she smiled, conscious of the increasing speed of her heartbeats, 'in case I run off with a few trees from your woodland, or a posse of animals from Hazel Farm?'

Scott rubbed her hand over his thigh, watching her through narrow eyes as he inched it higher. Was he testing her? she wondered, and tugged at her hand, saying hoarsely, 'Please stop it.'

He smiled as if he had proved a point, then tossed it back to her, rising and rubbing the back of his neck. Kirsten wondered if the night he had spent on the lounger in her room had taken its toll of his muscle-fitness.

'Arnie Smith's retiring.'

'He is? He didn't tell me. He knew I was still handling the estate——'

'He caught me in the village this morning. Told me then. Therefore,' Scott stretched luxuriously and the village shop's cotton shirt parted company with the waistband of the denims, revealing the whipcord leanness of his waist, 'Hazel Farm will cease to exist in a few months' time.'

He wandered back to the window.

'But why, Scott?' Kirsten asked. 'You could easily let it again.'

'Or sell it.'

Kirsten went cold. Three small words, but with a power packed into them that could change her life. 'The farm as a going concern, or the land it stands on?'

'Miss Ingram?' Cherry Marston's voice floated up the stairs. 'You still in bed?'

'Yes, Cherry, but I think I'll get up later.'

'Oh no, you won't.' Scott was standing over her. 'I've asked Cherry to come here—at my expense—to keep an eye on you. In half an hour, I'm going back to London. One or two appointments to keep, so,' he bent over her, 'you'll stay right there. Got it?'

'Scott,' impulsively she caught his wrist, feeling its strength, the soft hairs caught down by his watch, 'please don't sell Hazel Farm!'

He looked down at her fingers twining around his skin and a small smile played over his well shaped mouth. 'I don't mix emotion with business decisions, Kirsten,' he said softly.

'You mean,' she said with a bitterness she could not disguise, 'a banker has to do what he has to do.'

'As a businessman,' he emphasised the words, 'I shall do whatever is commercially viable.' He stared down at her hand until she released him.

There was that ring of authority in his voice again which she had noticed when she had first met him. A man, she had thought then, who would never give in to persuasion. Now she was better acquainted with him, she knew that her first impressions had been right.

He had not answered her question then as to whether or not he had agreed to sell his land to Samson Developments. Nor would he answer now if she were to repeat it.

'Can I come in?' Cherry stood at the door, an armful of

magazines almost spilling over. 'I got them, Mr Baird, all the ones on your list.'

He nodded his thanks and watched as Cherry lowered the pile of glossy magazines to the bed, adding with a smile, 'All for you, Miss Ingram.'

Surprised, Kirsten looked up at Scott. 'Why?'

'To give you ideas about redecoration and furnishings.' He smiled again, and there was a hint of challenge in his eyes. 'Let your imagination run wild.'

'Regardless of cost?'

'Money no object. Now,' he consulted his watch, 'regretfully, I must go. Back to work, back to civilisation.' He halted in the doorway. 'I'll be back. Make a note of your choice of furniture, colour combinations, kitchen equipment. Get the idea?' His smile turned her heart over.

The front door slammed, a car came to life and roared away.

'My,' sighed Cherry, 'what a man!' She looked out at the gravel his car tyres had scattered. 'I could fall for him, if I hadn't already got a man of my own.'

So could I, Kirsten thought, closing her eyes, and in a big way too. I already have, haven't I? she both asked and answered herself.

'What a lovely gesture, Miss Ingram—to say you could have whatever you wanted for your house!'

Kirsten smiled, suddenly weary, as though some of her life force had left with Scott Baird. 'It's only because I'm going to rent two or three rooms to him, Cherry. A man like that—it's difficult to imagine him living in anything but the best, isn't it?'

Cherry frowned, agreeing. 'I'd have thought the place was a bit tumbledown for the likes of Mr Baird.'

'Don't worry, he's going to have Tall Trees patched up. Fred Burns is going to do it, he said. Not quite as good as new, but so that it doesn't leak or flood or blow great gales around the windows and doors.'

'That'll be good for you, too, won't it?' Cherry frowned again. 'He'll be living here, then? Got a wife, has he?'

Kirsten could follow where Cherry's mind had leapt to—shared house, shared lives. 'No wife, Cherry. But he'll only be here weekends and holidays. And,' she smiled, 'he's a real gentleman, isn't he?' Have I reassured her? Kirsten wondered. 'I mean, he won't—he and I . . . He'll respect my privacy as much as I'll respect his. Don't you think?'

Cherry looked relieved. 'Especially as he's Mr Hazelton's great-nephew. There was one of his young relatives, Mr Hazelton used to tell me, that he liked above all the others. And he was the one, the old gentleman told me, that he'd remember in his will. Must have been that one.' She nodded towards the empty doorway, then bustled through it.

Kirsten picked up one of the glossies and turned the pages. Lennard Hazelton had mentioned a 'special great-nephew' to her too. 'He's grown into one of the best,' he had said. The best what? she wondered now. Best as a businessman or as a human being? She had, she decided, yet to discover the answer.

CHAPTER FIVE

FEELING much better a few days later, Kirsten ventured out into the sunshine. With a returning sense of well-being, she wandered around the orchard which lay just beyond the gardens of Tall Trees.

There had been no word from Scott, and she was beginning to wonder if he had changed his mind about becoming her tenant. If he had, she was forced to acknowledge that she would be bitterly disappointed.

All around her, the fruit trees, although displaying promising signs of a fruitful harvest to come, had a neglected, rather wild look about them. The fruit they had borne the previous autumn lay largely where it had fallen, overripe and unwanted.

In Mr Hazelton's later years, his estate seemed to have become too much for him to cope with, the orchard suffering the most from his lack of practical interest. The villagers had been invited in to take their pick but, even so, much of the fruit had been wasted.

The thought occurred to Kirsten that if she, as manager of the estate, could persuade Scott to employ a firm of gardening contractors to bring the orchard back to life, and maybe to profitability, he might then decide to preserve it and resist any offers for its purchase as a site for development.

Returning to the house, she realised with a sense of relief that, in her position as caretaker of the estate, she had the power to fight off any advances which Samson Developments might make to Scott for the purchase of his land.

Peter called in. He was on his way, he said, to visit a client.

'Would you believe,' he declared, grinning, 'that I caught the whiff of coffee all the way down the drive?' He sniffed around, like a dog following a scent trail.

'If that's not a hint,' Kirsten responded drily, 'then I don't know what is! If you want to talk, you'll have to come into the kitchen while I get the coffee ready.'

He sat on a wooden folding chair and put his feet up on a counter-top. 'What's this I hear, then,' he commented with a sly sideways look, 'about a tall, dark handsome banker coming to live with you?'

Kirsten swung round sharply. 'Who told you? Cherry?'

'So it's true. Kirsten,' he shook his head slowly in mock reprimand, 'I'm disappointed in you. Here am I, willing and eager to move in with you any time, do my bit in——' he looked around him '—filling in cracks and keeping out the raindrops, and you go behind my back and form a liaison with some millionaire type——'

'Look, Peter.' She pushed his feet to the ground and they hit the floor with a thump. 'One,' she counted on her fingers, 'it's true I've agreed to take on Scott Baird as a tenant. Two, as a tenant and *nothing else*. I'm surprised at you thinking otherwise. For heaven's sake,' she shoved the sugar-bowl towards him and he helped himself liberally, 'even if I were interested in him, which I'm not——' Well, she was, but where was the future in that? '—I'm way out of his league. Now do you understand?'

'Not entirely, but I'll believe you.' He took a swig of coffee and wiped his mouth as though it had been beer.

In his working suit, Peter was quite good-looking. Wasn't it a pity, Kirsten reflected, that it had to be Scott Baird she had fallen for, instead of an uncomplicated type like Peter?

'Was it sentiment that made him want to rent a room in

his late great-uncle's house?' Peter queried. 'Or does he think deep down, the place should have been left to him, along with the rest?'

'A simple straightforward wish for a weekend retreat, as far as I could gather.'

He put his head on one side. 'Not the enticing thought of the landlady in residence? When he saw me in your bedroom when you were ill, he looked as though he'd have liked to chuck me straight out of the crumbling old window!'

Kirsten felt the colour creep into her cheeks. The memory of Scott's gentleness when he had looked after her; the sweet but meaningless kisses they had exchanged; the way he had stayed beside her through the night—stirred a potent longing within her that she knew would never be assuaged.

'You mean,' she remarked lightly, 'that Scott Baird was acting the possessive male towards me?' She shook her head. 'Think again. He told me he felt responsible for me as his late great-uncle's "pet lamb". If he felt anything at all, it was probably a guilty conscience after turning me away from his presence earlier that day with the words "no loan" ringing in my ears.'

The telephone rang and, taking the call, she listened with growing surprise and pleasure to Mr Phipps' news, then ran back to the kitchen.

'Mr Stewartson, the bookseller, is buying the whole library,' she exclaimed, eyes shining, 'not just those first editions!' She told Peter the amount the man had agreed to pay and his eyes sprang open. 'He's got a client in mind, he said, so he could sell them again straight away.'

'That's a lot of cash,' said Peter, rising. 'I know a few of those volumes are worth quite a bit, but some of the others . . . But why should you worry? When are they collecting them? The library will look empty without them.'

'They're to stay where they are until further notice.'
Kirsten clasped her hands. 'All that money—I'll put it into
a savings account for——' She checked herself. She
couldn't confide in Peter, not yet anyway, about her plans
for Tall Trees. 'For the future.'

She walked with Peter to his car. 'I had a letter from
Marianne,' she told him. 'She's working in France for
another six months.'

'I know. The parents weren't very pleased. She's fallen
for her boss, but he's tied up with some glamorous female,
so no future there for her. Trust my sister to fall for the
wrong man!' He gave her a quick, knowing look. 'You
women are all the same. Even this glamorous female.' He
ruffled her hair. 'You spurn all the men within reach and
claw the air in a pointless effort to clutch fantasy men to
your shapely bosoms. You never learn, do you?'

He gave her a swift kiss on the cheek and drove away.

The morning's post lay untouched on the desk.
Reaching for a letter opener, Kirsten started on it. There
were notes from Baird estate tenants—Scott had inherited
an assortment of cottages in the village. There was a
magazine from a tree growers' association which she
skimmed through, and a handful of official communi-
cations.

Staring at the telephone on the desk, she wished for the
hundredth time that Scott would call. Since he had walked
out of her bedroom that morning, there had been no word
from him.

Even as she stared, it sprang to life, its ring shredding
the silence to pieces. Her hand shot out and, even before
she answered, she sensed it was Scott. Would she hold? his
secretary asked. Mr Baird would like a word.

'Kirsten, how are you?' His voice, deep and clear and
surprisingly warm, made her pulses break into a trot.

The tenderness in his tone shortened her breaths and she

answered jerkily, 'Much better now, thank you. And I haven't had a chance yet to say thanks for looking after me——'

'Only too happy,' he broke in, 'to be of use.' Just like that, she thought, trite words, a friendly gesture, no more, no less. But, she chided herself, hadn't she been the fool to have read more into his unexpected visit? Friendly concern for her was more like it, even a guilty conscience coming into operation, as she had told Peter.

'Sorry I haven't been in touch earlier,' he went on. 'I've been abroad for a few days. In a day or two—I wanted to warn you—you'll be having a call from Fred Burns. His quote for the repairs is acceptable, so I won't bother to obtain others. He's a local man, his reputation would suffer if he did a lousy job. How do you feel about that? It's your house, after all.' He read out the builder's estimate.

'Yes, but it's your money, Scott. I have heard the villagers praising his work, which must mean he's reliable.'

'Good. As soon as he's free of some other job he's on, he'll be calling round to fix a date for starting.' Scott paused, and his softened tone told Kirsten he was smiling. 'Made your list yet of new furniture and fresh décor?'

'Oh, yes!' she responded eagerly. 'I hope the cost won't shake you, but you did tell me to let my imagination off the leash.'

'And did you?'

'Mm, but within reason.'

'Ah, yes,' she was sure she could could hear him fiddling with a pen, 'always within reason. That's my rational, well balanced girl!'

His girl? Her heart danced, then reason took control. But she hadn't imagined that certain note in his voice—had she? Yes, she had. He had spoken with sarcasm, not possession!

'When will you be coming, Scott?' she asked.

'To commence my tenancy?' He gave a short laugh. 'We haven't decided yet, have we, which rooms I'm to have? Nor have we settled on the rent.'

'That doesn't matter.' Had she sounded too eager? She must make herself sound more businesslike. 'Come as a visitor first, get the feel of the rooms, the way they face——'

'Try them in rotation, you mean?' He sounded amused. 'It's a novel idea, I might take you up on it.' There was a pause, and Kirsten wondered if he was about to finish the conversation, but it seemed he had been deep in thought. Probably, she surmised, of how to word the statement he proceeded to make. 'I've had an offer for Hazel Farm.'

Her heart hit rock bottom. 'Please don't sell,' she renewed her plea. 'At least, not for building on. Graze the local riding school's horses on it, plant trees; rent it out to the village football team, turn it over to recreation. They're all good ideas, Scott.' He said nothing. 'But then, you're a businessman, aren't you?' she added bitterly. 'First, middle and last! And, as such, you make a point of getting your money's worth out of every transaction, regardless of the human cost.'

'Being sarcastic gets you nowhere, Kirsten,' he reprimanded quietly. 'If I see fit to sell land which is mine, for whatever purpose, that is my business entirely.'

'I manage your estate,' she blurted out. 'I could——' She mauled her bottom lip, but it was too late.

'You could what?' he rasped. 'Don't threaten me, Miss Ingram.' The slam of the receiver was painful to her ear.

Kirsten stared through the window, blinking away the tears. With her pleas and her defiance she had made things worse. She had challenged him and, like any other man of his calibre, he would surely rise to it.

Four days later, Kirsten knew that he had. A letter

addressed to her arrived, bearing the name of his bank. Her intuition warned her that the contents spelt trouble, and her fingers trembled as they opened it.

'Dear Miss Ingram,' the letter said, 'reference, Baird Estate. This is to inform you that, as from today, I am relieving you of the position of manager of my estate, having appointed a firm of professional estate managers to take over the work from you.

'In future,' the letter continued, 'would you please pass on to this firm'—he gave the name—'every item of correspondence which comes your way connected with the Baird estate.

'Finally, as promised,' it concluded, 'I am enclosing a cheque, made out to you personally, to cover the period of weeks since my late great-uncle's demise, during which you acted as manager of my estate.'

The cheque was for a large and, Kirsten had to admit, generous amount, but it did nothing to cool the heat of her anger at the step he had taken.

He was, she fumed, hard-headed and unfeeling, and she would throw his request to rent some rooms from her back in his implacable, handsome face. Reason tried to persude her that he had every right to dispose of his land as he liked, but she would not listen to it. He would, out of spite, she was sure, sell the land to the most ruthless, insensitive property developer he could find.

Then he would stand back and laugh at the way Tall Trees—and she herself—had been fenced in by a residential development of brick and concrete of unattractive design which would reach to the very edge of her property.

The amount of the cheque, she argued angrily, was just his conscience talking. He knew as well as she did that, before long, her house and garden would lose its identity—and, incidentally, much of its resale value—because of his decision to sell Hazel Farm—and who knew how much else of his land?—to the highest bidder.

And, worst of all, since she had now been replaced as his estate manager, she had no control at all over events concerning the environs of her house and garden.

There was the sound of the back door opening. Knowing that it was not Cherry's day for coming, Kirsten hazarded that it might be the local builder who had knocked and she had not heard him.

'Mr Burns?' she called out. 'I've been expecting you. I'm here in the room Mr Hazelton used as his study, remember? I——'

'Kirsten.'

She swung round, her body tingling as though she had touched a live wire.

'How did you get in?' She knew her tone was accusing and entirely lacking in the polite welcome she should have given such a visitor, but she felt neither polite nor welcoming at that moment towards Scott Baird. His letter of dismissal was in her hand, and it was as much as she could do not to squeeze it into a paper ball and hurl it at him.

He looked her over and, despite the appreciation she could detect in his eyes, she burned with indignation—and something else that only he could arouse in her.

'I rang the bell, but no one came, so I tried the kitchen door and here I am.' He saw the letter in her hand. 'How are you?'

'As you can see, better, thank you. Despite the contents of this.' Kirsten waved it in the air. 'It's a reflection on my integrity!' she accused. 'Did you think I wouldn't be able to put my personal feelings behind me and be completely detached in dealing with the sale of your land?'

'Despite the fact that it would be against your own interests? Come now, Kirsten,' he strolled in, 'you're only human. If you'd continued as manager, be honest, wouldn't you have been tempted to put as many difficulties in the way as possible? I'd have understood it if you had, but I would have been furious. Some time you would have had to go. Better now than with recriminations and anger later.'

'So now you're making out, are you, that you're the good guy, while I'm the baddie? This cheque——' She thrust it out.

'Well?' His tone, and his eyes, were cold. 'Isn't it enough?' He felt in his inner pocket and produced his cheque-book and pen. 'You want more?'

'*More?*' she cried. 'What kind of a woman do you think I am? *This* is too much. I'd tear it up and throw it back at you, but I need it so badly. I'll put it with my savings,' she told him, feeling a deep satisfaction at having found a way of getting back at him somehow, 'and add to it over the months. You see, I've started a fund.' She smiled with a feeling of triumph. 'Towards the conversion of Tall Trees into the retirement residence Mr Hazelton—and I—had dreamed about.'

Narrow-eyed, Scott stared at her, then he shrugged his broad shoulders. 'As you wish. If it's going to make you happy, carry on with your dreams. But face facts, Kirsten. A project like that would cost thousands. Where's the rest coming from?'

'I'll think of something. Peter will help me. And his sister, when she comes back to this country.'

'So your boyfriend's a mini-millionaire? And generous with it, too? But then,' his gaze raked her, and she was sure he was undressing her in his imagination, 'who wouldn't be, with you dangling yourself on a string in front of him?'

She lifted her hand to hit out, but he caught it and she winced at his grip.

'Don't insult me!' she exclaimed angrily. 'F-first you

attack my integrity, now you question my morals!' She bit her lip to help her withstand his bruising hold. 'Peter's pleasant and nice. He's an architect, but he's young and has a long way to go, careerwise. Which means he's certainly not rich.'

He must have seen her pain, since he relented, releasing her, but the set of his jaw stayed inflexible.

'The question remains,' he averred. 'Sit down and do your sums. The amount of cash an idea like yours will need to finance it isn't remotely within your reach. Ask your architect boyfriend.'

'He's already told me his opinion. To forget it.'

'So he's got some sense.'

'Meaning, I suppose, that in taking up with me, he's lacking in it?'

Scott's eyelids drooped as his gaze travelled speculatively over the swelling shape and curves of her body, lifting to the rich brown of her hair, coming to rest on the echoing brown of her eyes. 'Did I say so?'

'You didn't have to. The implication was there.'

Kirsten turned away, but he took a few steps and caught her arm, impelling her towards him. She tried to shake off his hand, but it was only a token effort; she liked the touch of him too much for her peace of mind.

'You're very attractive, Kirsten. I wouldn't blame any man for wanting an affair with you.'

She did jerk away then, rubbing her arm. 'I'm not in the market for an affair. What is it you want, Scott? Still angling for this house? That's not on the market, either. How many times do I have to tell you it's not for sale before you'll believe it?'

'You there, Mr Baird?'

Fred Burns' footsteps sounded hesitant as they advanced along the hallway towards Mr Hazelton's old study. 'I thought I heard your voice. Oh, sorry, miss.' He turned to go, but Kirsten called him back. Looking from one to the other, Fred lifted his cap and scratched his head.

'Go ahead, Mr Burns,' Kirsten invited. 'Talk to Mr Baird. I'm so pleased you'll be working on the house.'

'Well, you couldn't go on living in this cold, damp building, Miss Ingram, not without waterproofing it and keeping out the 'orrible weather we get in the wintertime. Catch your death, you would.'

'She nearly did, Fred,' Scott remarked drily. 'Told me she'd got a hangover.'

'Never!' He shook his head at Kirsten.

'What she'd really got,' Scott went on, 'was a bad attack of bronchitis, which almost turned into something worse.'

Fred shook his head slowly. 'If you'd told my good lady, miss, she'd have been up here like a shot and looked after you.'

'Thanks for that, Mr Burns,' said Kirsten, smiling, 'but I managed. Cherry came extra days and——' She glanced at Scott and wondered whether he would be annoyed if she mentioned him. 'And Mr Baird came, too. Which,' she overcame her anger with him enough to admit, 'was very kind of him.'

'I just didn't believe her story,' he took her up, which she realised confirmed that he had not minded her mentioning him, 'so I decided to check up on her. Which was lucky, because she was fit to drop when I arrived.'

'I'd heard you'd——' Mr Burns corrected himself quickly, 'someone had stayed a night or two.' He glanced from one to the other again, his eyes asking the question for him, but his mouth closed on the query.

There's nothing like that between us, Kirsten wanted to say, but Scott broke in, plainly to set the record straight, 'She was my great-uncle's assistant for some years, Mr Burns, so,' his eyes swung to her enigmatically, 'since he isn't here any more to make sure she takes care of herself, I decided that it would be his wish that I should make myself responsible for her welfare.'

Fred Burns nodded, apparently understanding now. Plainly, any suspicions he might have had about a possible relationship between his two companions had been banished by Scott's carefully chosen words.

But Scott had only stated the truth, Kirsten told herself. Those few kisses when he had been looking after her had held no meaning. And, if her heart took a tumble at her mind's dismissal of Scott's concern about her when she had been ill, then, she argued, it was time for her to face reality. There would never be a time when she would mean anything to this man.

'I've got me mate outside, Mr Baird,' said Fred. 'He's only a youngster, but he's bright and he needed a job. Now, where should we start?'

Scott turned to Kirsten and his eyebrows indicated that he wanted her opinion. 'The roof, Kirsten?'

'Oh yes, please. It's leaking in so many places, it's a bit like a sieve!'

'The roof it is, Fred,' said Scott, going out with him.

Their voices faded and a door swung behind them. In the silence that followed, Kirsten's thoughts echoed loudly, reminding her that the job she had enjoyed had been taken away from her, and all because Scott had not trusted her to be impartial over the management of his private affairs.

Through the window she watched him as he stood with Mr Burns, hands on his hips, head back, jet-black hair tossed by the breeze, gazing up at the roof. His broad shoulders pushed at his dark, jersey-knit shirt, his hands on hips that were moulded by the good cut of the casual trousers he wore.

Even as she looked at him, Kirsten felt again that strange pulling sensation, as though something inside him had lassoed her with a length of rope on which he had only to tug and she was there at his side. Every time she heard his voice, or looked into his eyes, her heart did a double somersault, and there was absolutely nothing she could do to stop it.

For the next half-hour she went systematically through Mr Hazelton's filing cabinets, pulling out every folder and file relating to the estate his great-nephew had inherited.

There was a noise at the door and her head swung round. She rose, her face flushed with effort and a barely suppressed anger.

'There you are,' she declared, gesturing to the cardboard boxes she had filled, 'every communication, memo, bill and receipt I can find. Pass this lot over to the *experts on estate management*! Then you'll be able to rest easy in your bed at night, knowing your estate's in *safe, professional* hands and not at the mercy of a bungling amateur who'd put personal feelings before business and——'

Three strides brought him across the room, and his hands gripped her arms. 'All I'm doing is taking a load off your shoulders. And you know it!'

Shaking free, Kirsten tugged at her cotton top, annoyed at once with herself for doing so since it brought Scott's attention downwards to her shapeliness.

'What load?' she challenged. 'It wasn't a load when I acted as manager for your great-uncle. With his guidance, I dealt with it all—the care of the woodland, the three farms, the fencing and the hedging. Not to mention the cottages that go with the estate.'

'*With his guidance.* They're three important words, Kirsten. If I were to let you carry on as manager——'

'You think,' she broke in, 'that I'd be on the phone to

you every five minutes to get *your* guidance? You couldn't be more wrong. I know enough about it now to be able to deal with everything but the really big decisions. And I *would* have done the work impartially, whatever you might say now. It would have gone against the grain, of course it would, but I'd have *made* myself objective in dealing with the property developers or whoever.'

'And,' he took her up, his voice hard, 'resentment would have built up in you to such an extent that you'd have grown to hate the man who had forced the situation on you.'

'Hate?' She frowned, her eyes drawn to his daunting physique, the way his strong shoulders pushed impatiently at his shirt. His inky-black hair swept downward over his brow and her fingers itched to push it back into place.

'Hate?' she repeated, with a deliberately negligent movement of her head. 'I doubt if I could feel *any* kind of strong emotion towards you,' she lied, 'let alone that.'

It gave her a flick of pleasure to see Scott's mouth tighten at her words, but the sensation was short-lived. The feelings she really had for this man were worryingly potent. She would much rather bring a smile to his face than irritation, desire to his expression than dismissal . . . But where would that get her?

He walked to the window and stared out, hands thrust into trouser pockets. What were his thoughts? Kirsten wondered. If only there had not been this sudden chill in their relations! Where was that warmth, the compatibility that had existed between them, if only for a day or two, when he had cared for her during her illness?

'Would it have mattered all that much,' she commented, making her tone flippant, 'even if I had grown to hate you?'

She steeled herself for a derisive lift of his shoulders and was disconcerted when instead he answered with deep seriousness, 'It would have mattered.'

'Scott? she asked faintly.

He turned slowly and came towards her, stopping a couple of paces away. His eyes went to her thick, dark hair, lingering on the almost perfect oval of her face, then rested on her wide, generous mouth. It was, Kirsten thought, her heart racing, as if he were kissing her with his eyes. Her lips trembled faintly, as if his mouth was about to come down on them.

To her intense disappointment, he made no move to close the gap that separated them.

'Would you show me these rooms you're intending to lease to me?' he asked.

At his matter-of-fact tone, her heartbeats steadied. Her defensive mechanism came into play and she became down-to-earth too.

'Of course.' She put on her most businesslike tone. 'Take your pick. There are at least twenty to choose from. Upstairs or down?'

'Up, I think.' He followed her to the stairs and she talked as she climbed.

'I expect you know the layout of the house by now, after staying here for a couple of days.'

'It's engraved on my mind,' he commented drily. 'The bedroom I got the blanket from will be quite acceptable as a place to sleep.' They were walking side by side along the corridor. 'I believe there's an adjacent room which might at some time be converted into an en-suite bathroom.'

'You're wiling to spend that amount of money on the place?'

'Why so surprised?' queried Scott, smiling faintly. 'You've surely got me labelled as a man who likes his creature comforts?'

'Perhaps I have, but not as someone who's willing to throw his money away. After all,' she gave him a sarcastic sideways glance, 'it wasn't so long ago that you were telling me that all Tall Trees was fit for was demolition.'

'The repairs I'm paying for,' he pointed out briskly, 'are mere first aid on a property which is still being occupied, and therefore has to be made fit for human habitation. Having a room fitted out as a bathroom might seem an extravagance to you, but——' his eyes contemplated her profile '—as you would be the first to agree, I'm not exactly poverty-stricken.'

Something in her died—expectation, hope that his expenditure of money on her house implied a certain commitment, although to what she did not know. He had made it brutally plain that he had no more than a passing interest in the place, and that the financial outlay was, to him, so minute that it scarcely registered as a decimal point on the small fortune he seemed to have amassed over the years.

Whatever it was, disappointment made her adrenalin rise. She halted outside one of the rooms and flashed him a look that would have crushed a lesser man.

'There really was no need, Mr Baird,' she fumed, 'to make it so brutally plain that you have no more than a passing interest in my house. Or that the financial outlay you're making on it is so minuscule to you that it hardly registers as a decimal point on the small fortune you seem to possess!'

Sparks spat in his steely gaze, and Kirsten thought she had gone too far. Then twin golden flares turned his brown eyes to a warm amber and the tiny knot of fear that had formed inside her slowly loosened.

He leant a shoulder against the door jamb, pushing his hands into his pockets and crossing his long legs. 'You'd prefer me to have more than a *passing* interest in Tall Trees?' His gaze slid down her figure, then up again, bumping over the swell of her breasts, which they seemed curiously reluctant to leave, then back to her face. He could not have missed its heightened colour as he commented, a slight drawl in his voice, 'For that to happen, I'd have to have *more than a passing interest* in its owner.'

'If by that,' she hit back immediately, her heart sinking because once again they were on the verge of a quarrel, 'you're hinting that, if we were to have an affair, you'd *pour* money into the place, then you're wasting your breath! First,' her right forefinger hit the palm of her left hand, 'I won't be bought. Second,' her finger came down again, 'I can only repeat that my body's not on offer, any more than the house is.'

Fire burned in her cheeks, and she swung past him into the bedroom. 'This,' she announced, staring at the modest furnishings as if they had done her some terrible wrong, 'is the room you mentioned. You said it would suit——' She glanced at him and, to her chagrin, saw that his mouth was curved into a smile which was, she knew, at her expense.

Scott lifted himself upright and, instead of following her, moved out into the corridor and into the empty room next door. Curious now, Kirsten heard him rapping with his knuckles on the adjoining wall.

'Solid, darn it,' he cursed, 'built like a bloody fortress.'

'What else did you expect?' she queried triumphantly, watching him from the door. 'If anyone ever tried—over my dead body—to demolish Tall Trees, it would probably break the bulldozer first.'

'Don't,' he cautioned, brows drawn together, 'push your luck. I could withdraw my offer to patch up your precious property just like that.' He clicked his fingers at her.

Her colour flared again, furious with him for his veiled threat. 'No one blackmails me, *Mr Baird*!' she threw at him. 'You know what you can do with your money, don't you?' Her finger pointed stiffly towards the top of the staircase. 'You also know where the front door is. Goodbye, Mr Baird!'

CHAPTER SIX

A COUPLE of strides and Scott's hands were grasping Kirsten's underarms, jerking her so that her breasts were crushed against his chest. The steel was back in his eyes, his mouth pulled into a tight, ferocious line.

'And no one,' he said thickly, 'shows me the door and gets away with it. Least of all a young woman with a challenge in every look she throws at me, defiance in every sinuous, sexy curve.' His palms ran boldly down, indenting into her waist, pressing lower to her hips and thighs, returning to cup the provocative thrust of her breasts. 'She gets exactly what she asks for, which is this.'

His arms took a punishing hold of her tense body, while his mouth crushed hers, slowly but irresistibly pushing her backwards until her hands were forced to find a hold on the concrete hardness of his biceps in order to save herself from falling.

His mouth had by now forced her lips apart, and he was proceeding to make himself totally familiar with the taste of her. As her mouth gave up its secrets under the persistence of his plundering, so her body melted and her limbs turned to water. She had never been kissed so possessively before, almost to the point of submission, and it stirred to aching life feelings which, until that moment, she had not even been aware she had.

Not just any man could do this to her. Robin had often kissed and held her, yet she had never felt this driving need to cling, to hold on, to join her life and body—to *this* man's body. *And no other man's* . . .

Dazed, she stared up at him. He looked into her face; at her mouth that throbbed so much she was sure he could see its tremulous movement, at the sweep of her brow, then finally into her wondering eyes.

Voices were raised outside. Mr Burns was giving instructions to his novice builder's mate. There was a short burst of hammering, then a muffled curse as the hammer landed in the wrong place.

'Go inside, Tommy,' Kirsten heard Fred Burns advise with exaggerated patience, 'and ask the young lady for a plaster.'

'It's all right,' muttered Tommy. 'Didn't draw blood.'

Amused by the exchange, Kirsten smiled into Scott's eyes, loving the sensation of his arms around her, of being so close she could catch the scent of his lotion, see a close-up view of the darker, shaved area of his face. He smiled down, and their shared amusement joined them in a familiarity almost as deep as that of the kiss that had linked them.

'We-e-ll . . .' he said, the word drawn out, his expelled breath fanning the sensitive skin around her lips, 'if ever a man struck gold . . .' His hand lifted a stray tendril back into place. 'Robin doesn't know what he's missing!'

She stiffened in his arms, wanting to move away. Scott sensed her inclination, but would not let her go. What had she expected, she asked herself, when his kiss had merely been intended as a punishment for her audacity in showing him the door?

'Now what's wrong?' he asked softly, feeling her tension.

'Did you have to be cynical about something that— that——'

His thumb stroked her brow while his other arm held

her to him.

'Something that——?' He waited, his mouth held a mere caress away from hers.

'That——' Meant so much to me, Kirsten was thinking, but could not say without giving her secrets away.

It seemed he couldn't wait for her answer. His mouth was back on target, his embrace suffocatingly tight, yet she revelled in his closeness, feeling the sinewy toughness of his thighs pressing against hers.

When her arms crept around his neck, she did not call them to order, and when her lips started returning his kisses, she did not care that they were telling him far more than words could ever say.

As he lifted his head, she could only rest her cheek against his chest and stare wordlessly up at him. Her ear picked up his heart's hard pounding, heard his quickened, indrawn breaths. She made to move, and this time his arms gave her her freedom.

Going to the window, trying to recover, she watched the two men at work outside.

'Will this room——' She was forced to clear the hoarseness from her throat. 'Will this room be suitable for conversion into a bathroom?'

'It has distinct possibilities,' was his easy answer. There was a drawl in his voice and she was sure he was laughing at her. Why? she agonised. For taking so seriously something that was to him a mere passing indulgence?

'Good.' She turned briskly and found his thoughtful gaze upon her, his mouth formed into that faint, maddening curve. Come what may, she vowed, she would be businesslike with this man. Play him at his own game, that was what she would do, she resolved. Let him believe that to her, as to him, a kiss was just a kiss.

Her smile was superficial and efficient. 'So you think Mr Burns will be able to find a hammer big enough to make a hole in the wall?'

'Tunnel his way through, is more like it. Now,' hands in his pockets, Scott looked around, 'I'll need a living-room, plus another bedroom.' His eyebrows lifted at her change of expression. 'For a guest.'

'Of course.' Had her bracing tone disguised the dip her spirits had taken at the vision of his latest woman coming to stay? 'The next one along from yours?' If she hadn't smiled, she thought, she would by now be baring her teeth.

'Why not?' he answered casually, and wandered out, looking right and left. 'That one.' It was opposite her own, and she knew that he knew this. The thought of lying in bed, listening to his girl friend creeping along the corridor to her host's bedroom, or vice versa, almost made her shriek at him to stop torturing her like this!

The room was empty of furniture and, large as it was, it echoed as their footsteps advanced. The sun, which had come from behind the clouds, streamed in. I hope it gives hell to his woman, Kirsten thought furiously, when she wakes up late after a hangover and a night of love!

'Will you need the next room along,' she asked over-sweetly, 'for a bathroom conversion, too? For your—er— guest's convenience, naturally.'

'That depends,' his eyes swung back to her, 'on the wishes of my future landlady.'

'You mean, how willing I would be to allow my property to be manhandled——'

'Modified would be a better word,' he inserted.

'Messed around with,' she insisted, 'by a tenant who's merely passing through?'

'I could take exception to your slightly insulting phraseology,' returned Scott, not without menace, 'but I won't. Perhaps I should point out that any alterations I might make would contribute in a very material way to that dream which, for some inexplicable reason, you seem to cherish.' He had deliberately put her on the defensive and she started to protest, when he added, 'I don't think you really appreciate the enormous cost of carrying out such a project.'

Letting out a sigh, Kirsten stayed silent on the subject. She was not going to argue with him over something about which her mind was firmly made up. But his point that the alterations and repairs would contribute towards the realisation of her dream was a valid one.

Following this thought through, there was a request she particularly wanted to make. 'Could you, do you think——?' she ventured, moistening her lips with the darting point of her tongue. He watched the movement, eyes narrowed. 'Would it be possible, Scott, for me to have a—an adjoining bathroom to my bedroom too?'

His laughter burst from him at her impudence. 'Why not? Anything's possible if you've got the money. Would you dip into your savings?' An eyebrow lifted, his smile was a taunt.

'My savings?' He had misunderstood! She watched him nervously, like a mouse between two cats. Was his mood soft enough? Was her coaxing persuasive enough? Or would his great paw come down and squash her? 'I——' She put her head winningly on one side. 'I did hope that you might——'

'That *I* might? You mean, at *my* expense?' His grin told her he had known all along what she had meant. 'That I spend *my* money on making you more comfortable? Now, that depends.' His raking gaze told her what it depended on.

How could she crush him—and his hopes? Or were they intentions? The way her heart leapt at the thought of an affair with him made her own anger turn about and snap at her.

This man, she told herself firmly, was the enemy. He was after her property for his own gain, and this was something she must not forget, no matter how deeply her emotions had become enmeshed with him. For her own sake, she must harden her heart to his very male attractiveness and his irresistible charm—when he cared to use it.

'Considering you're a businessman, Mr Baird,' she commented loftily, determined to deflate him, 'I expected a balanced, reasoned response from your intellect, not a lecherous reaction from your carnal reflexes!'

Anger flared fiercely in the deep brown of his eyes, then it vanished into the astonished laughter that shook his frame. 'W-ow,' he remarked, drawing out the word on a long breath, 'if we were in the boxing ring together, I'd be flat on my back! Round one to you, Miss Ingram.' His admiration now was all for her face, the intelligence that shone from it, the fire that still burned in her cheeks. 'You're the kind of female opponent I've come across in my dreams, but never, until now, in reality—with the fight in her of a tigress, and beautiful and brainy with it. You want to deal with the strictly business side of me?' His change of mood was swift and deadly. 'Right.' He put a distance between them and surveyed her, hands in his pockets, expression detached now and icy cool.

Kirsten shivered inside. What was coming? What had she done in trying to put Scott Baird—a man of his status and calibre—in his place?

'Having listened to my plans,' he said through taut lips, 'for the conversion of a couple of rooms in your house to cater for my own requirements, you're apparently now hoping to play on my sympathies and coax out of me a similar enhancement of your own living standards *at my expense*. I'm a businessman, Kirsten, as you've just pointed out, and as such, I'm giving you the answer. You're offering me no collateral, damn all in return. So that answer is no.'

Her lower lip began to quiver, but she fought back, tight-reining her emotions. 'I could refuse permission for you to do those conversions.'

'Do that,' he grated, 'and I would immediately withdraw from the arrangement.'

He had called her bluff! 'You mean, call the whole thing off? You wouldn't rent any of my rooms?'

Slowly he approached, menace in every line. 'I'm sorely tempted to tell you what you can do with your rented accommodation.'

'Coffee, Miss Ingram,' Cherry sang from downstairs. 'Will you have it in the kitchen like you usually do, or——'

The cheery voice broke the tension like an elastic band snapping.

'In the study, Cherry,' Kirsten called, hearing the giveaway waver in her own voice. 'I'll have it while I work. I've been delayed——'

'OK, Miss Ingram. Mr Baird still with you? Where'll he have his, then?'

'In the kitchen,' shouted Scott, 'with Fred and Tommy.'

'Scott?' Anger still roughened his eyes as he waited for Kirsten's question. 'Have you really changed your mind about renting those rooms from me?'

'Have you changed your mind about having me as a

tenant?'

She looked away, then back. 'I'd welcome the extra cash the rental would bring in.'

'You've no other source of income?'

'None at all, Scott.'

'Then we'll have to draw up a contract, won't we?' He smiled at the relief in her eyes, and added on a faintly sarcastic note, 'On a strictly *business* basis, of course.'

Her heart singing in competition with the birds outside, Kirsten followed him down the stairs.

Kirsten lunched alone. Cherry had cooked a light meal, having asked first if 'company' was expected to join her.

Kirsten searched everywhere for that 'company', even wandering into the orchard in search of him—all in vain. Nor was there any sign of Fred Burns and Tommy.

'Gone to the Three White Horses, I wouldn't be surprised,' concluded Cherry with a knowing smile.

Scott Baird, international banker, Kirsten thought unbelievingly, gone to the village pub for a drink and a sandwich? 'I doubt it, Cherry,' she commented firmly. 'Probably taken himself to the Moated Castle for a four-course meal with wine.

Back at her desk, she heard his voice and all the nerves in her body bristled as if they had been stroked the wrong way. Even her fingers, poised over the keys, trembled a little before she hammered each of them down.

'I thought you had,' she heard Cherry say with emphasis. 'Miss Ingram, she thought you'd gone to eat with the high-and-mighty lot in the town.'

'Oh, did she?' he asked, in a I'll-teach-her-to-think-that-of-me voice.

He stood in the doorway, arms folded, legs slightly apart. There was belligerence in every line of him, and Kirsten, who swivelled to greet him, remembered with alarming clarity the impact his kisses had made on her senses that morning. Her lips parted involuntarily, as if he were at that very moment about to repeat the exercise.

'So you think I'm incapable of descending to the level of the ordinary man?' Scott moved into the room, and her breathing became just a little shallower. 'You've classed me as a snob, have you, your knowledge of my character, of course, being so comprehensive?'

In spite of her heart's quickened beat, she retorted, 'Well, you don't exactly live on the poverty-line, do you? I mean, I wasn't really thinking in terms of your social compatibility with the everyday folk around you, but of the power of money.' He was bristling now, but she went doggedly on. 'I mean,' she qualified for the second time, doing her best to stroke his fur the right way again, 'if you can afford to order caviar and champagne, then why should you content yourself with something as mundane as cheese sandwiches and beer in a stuffy, smoke-filled local pub?'

Had she appeased him, scrubbed out his annoyance at her apparently mistaken interpretation of his character? She did not know, since he came, one slow, menacing stride after another, across the room. With an attempt at self-preservation she turned back to her typing, but he was not diverted from his intention.

From behind, an arm encircled her neck and her head was pulled back. Helpless, she was forced to stare up into glittering eyes and a downward-curving mouth above a thrusting jaw. 'Apologise,' he rasped, 'for those nasty slurs on my character. Say you're sorry, or——' he gave a slight jerk as her lips parted on a soundless gasp.

'I'm sorry, I didn't mean to insult you.' The words came in a rush, intoned on one note in her hurry to placate him.

'Right. Now kiss me.' Without haste, his mouth lowered, fixing diagonally across hers. The scent of alcohol invaded her nostrils and she could swear it was intoxicating her, robbing her of her ability to resist him. Her hands came up to pull at his imprisoning arm, but they rested there instead. His domination was carrying her away, depriving her of her will to remove his power over her.

With his free hand, Scott swivelled her chair, bringing her to face him, his arm moving to lift her supple body and enfold it in his arms. Her quivering lips parted, impatient for his to reclaim them. They were strangely dry and needed the warmth and persuasiveness of his mouth to bring them to life again.

'Scott,' she breathed, 'I——'

'You do?' His faint smile lowered and captured her unspoken words, although what she would have said if he had given her the chance she did not know.

This time he set her whole body alight, his hand more possessive now, loosening her cotton top and sliding under it in an upward stroking motion. Then it encountered the softness it had been seeking.

His fingers pushed aside the piece of lace and satin that enclosed the full, warm flesh, then moulded and caressed until she clung to his shoulders, his neck, wherever she could find a hold, pressing her body against his and giving him kiss for passionate kiss.

At last it was over, but her legs were so weak she could only lie back against his arm, drugged by his kisses, gazing into his glinting eyes. Then, in an uprush of emotion—a curious sensation of belonging for ever right where she was—she rested her face against his chest, hearing his heart's pounding and inhaling the clean masculine scent of him.

Raised voices invaded her little paradise—Cherry carrying on a joking conversation with Mr Burns; Tommy whistling tunelessly. It was the world outside reminding her of its existence, telling her that it was real, and that the heaven across whose borders she had strayed existed only in her mind: worse, her imagination.

Scott had been amusing himself, whereas she had been playing for keeps. If she had been foolish enough not just to give him her love, but her heart too, then, she thought ruefully, more fool her!

Disentangling herself, she put her hands to her flushed cheeks, half turning from him. He took away her hands and tilted her chin, looking into her eyes, but she kept them lowered, holding on to the secret which his merest glance at them would pick up.

He let her go, saying abruptly, 'I'll get my things from the car.'

'You're staying the night?'

'A few days, probably. Do you mind?'

'Of course not.' Kirsten's voice was as expressionless as his. The passion they had shared had gone. It wasn't even hanging in the air like a soft mist, promising to descend again at a moment's notice. 'The room you chose before—will that suit?'

'It'll be fine.' Stilted words, like a guest to a hotel manager.

As Scott returned from his car, she approached along the hall. 'Need any help?' she enquired politely. 'You look like an octopus!'

He was laden with cases, bulging folders, long, thin rolls of paper which resembled architect's plans. He laughed, at ease now.

'Thanks, but no. There are a few odd boxes to come, but they're too heavy for you.'

'I don't mind. I'm not a weakling.' She made to pass him, but his leg came out.

'Oh no, you don't! Are you always so darned obstinate?'

Kirsten's smile lit her face. 'I'm never obstinate.'

'Just plain stubborn, mm?'

She smiled, getting the feeling that, if his arms had not been fully occupied, they might have slid round her again. She forced her thoughts outwards to everyday matters.

'The list you suggested I make, Scott, of the furnishings and kitchen equipment . . .' He stopped half-way up the stairs. 'They add up to a lot of money.'

'That worries you? Is this a miracle?' He smiled mockingly down at her. 'A woman who worries about how much of a man's money she's intending to spend? You must surely be unique!' He continued walking. At the top he called down, 'Show me the list. Maybe this evening?'

Of course, he'd be there that evening! She nodded, turning back with apparent calm to her work. Scott was going to live in her house for the next few days . . . She would be hearing him around, meeting him just anywhere. The wonderful sensation of simply knowing he was there . . . Feeling as she did about him, how would her peace of mind stand up to that?

Peter called in as Kirsten prepared the evening meal.

'Smells good,' he remarked, following her into the kitchen. Her heart sank. What was she to do with him? She had been so looking forward to her evening with Scott, skimming through magazines, studying price lists.

Just before Peter had arrived, she had been going to ask Scott if he would like to share her meal.

'Hey,' said Peter, closing the kitchen door, 'whose fancy Saab is that in the drive? Come into some money?'

'It's Scott's—Scott Baird's.' Peter's eyebrows almost hit his hairline. 'He's here.'

'Doing what?' Then his face changed. 'Hey, you're not——? You two aren't——?'

'No, we're not,' Kirsten replied decisively. Well, they weren't, were they? So he'd kissed her—beautifully, fantastically—all of which meant precisely nothing, to Scott. 'Believe it or not, he's my tenant. He asked if he could rent a couple of rooms.'

'And for once you didn't say no.'

'Why should I? He hasn't propositioned me. It's a straightforward business arrangement.'

'OK, so I'll believe you. But others won't. Aren't you afraid of what people might say?'

'Why should I be? There'll be absolutely nothing for them to talk about.'

Peter shrugged, the action saying that it was her problem. 'Going to ask me to share your meal?'

Despair made Kirsten's eyes flicker shut. It was an appeal she could not refuse. How could she say that she was going to invite her new tenant . . .

Footsteps descended the stairs. The utensils Kirsten was using clattered down and she hurried into the hall. Peter followed more slowly. 'Scott, about this evening——' He had seen Peter and his smile faded. 'You do know, Scott, don't you, that the tenancy includes share of the kitchen and bathroom? If you want to cook your evening meal——'

'Thanks, no.' His voice was as cool as his eyes. 'I'm

told there's a three-star hotel in the town.'

'The Moated Castle,' Peter supplied cheerfully. 'Excellent cuisine. Prices to go with it.' His flat, raised hand indicated a point above his head.

Scott nodded, fastening a button of his lightweight jacket.

'Those lists we were going to look at, Scott——'

He had gone. If he'd heard her, he had given no sign. His car sprang to life and sped away, shifting gravel.

'So, who's in a bad mood, then?' joked Peter. 'The car or the driver?' Kirsten dropped a saucepan and retrieved it, exclaiming under her breath. 'Or maybe it's the cook?' he added with a sly grin.

Kirsten let the gibe go, angry inside, yet upset at the same time that once again Scott should have misjudged her relationship with Peter. It was obvious he had by the way he had looked at Peter, then slid the scowl across to her. There she was, his eyes had accused, entertaining another man, after letting him, Scott, kiss her with passion, and responding likewise. In doing so, in his book, she had made an unspoken offer—an offer which, if he had taken it up, would have led to the inevitable.

The trouble was, Kirsten thought, lowering a sizzling lamb chop on to a bed of tasty salad, that deep down it was that 'inevitable' step that her mind and—she could not deny it —her body wanted with a desperation that shocked her.

Peter stayed so long, she began to worry that Scott might return and find him still there. Suggesting a walk in the garden as a way at least of getting him out of the house, she beckoned him through the kitchen door and round the sideway.

Tall Trees, its impressive construction telling of past glories, never mind the present sad deterioration, was bathed in the gold-red of the late spring evening sun. There was a chill in the air, and Kirsten shivered, wishing she had collected a jacket on the way out. Peter put his arm round her waist and pulled her to his side.

'I'll warm you,' he said, and his smile was so sweet she did not have the heart to withdraw. 'Have you heard,' he remarked after a while, 'that Arnie Smith's giving up the tenancy of Hazel Farm?'

'I've heard,' she answered on a groan. Peter's eyebrows asked, who told you? 'The big boss himself. He also informed me he'd had an offer for it.'

'Oh? Who's the potential buyer?'

'Don't know—he didn't elaborate. Of course,' she glared up at him, 'you would be interested! An architect's always eager for work, isn't he, gobbling up the landscape with buildings and yet more buildings . . .?'

Peter pretended to take cover, without relinquishing his hold on her waist. 'Hey there, lady, I'm not your target! It's them thar' property developers you ought to be shouting at, not me. I do my best to make the buildings I design recede prettily into the landscape, with trees around, and if there aren't any trees, I have them planted.'

'You've made your point. Sorry, Peter. But I feel strongly about it.'

'Ma'am,' he joked, 'you certainly do! And,' he peered ahead, past the flowering shrubs and over the lawns which needed mowing, to the land beyond, 'if Hazel Farm went under bricks and mortar——'

'Not to mention the orchard, which Scott owns too.'

'You'd be hemmed in.'

There was a sad silence which, after a while, was broken by the sound of voices. 'You've got company,' said Peter in a low tone, 'and guess who?'

'It's Scott!' Kirsten hissed, recognising the deep tones. 'Why is he wandering about the orchard at this time of day?'

'He's not alone. There's a guy with him, pointing at the trees.'

'Oh no! He's not—he's not going to sell that, too! Peter, I couldn't stand it. Houses right up to the boundary of my beautiful gardens . . .'

He put both his arms round her waist, easing her to face him. 'Don't jump to conclusions. He might just be getting gardening advice.'

'And dogs might purr and cats might bark! If I know Scott Baird——'

'Do you?' Peter's voice was quiet, yet wanting to know.

'Not that way, stupid,' Kirsten reprimanded. If only she did! 'But he's a businessman through and through—I have it from source. I could,' she ground her teeth, *"slaughter* him! Come on, Peter, back to the house. I can't stand watching him put on the smooth sales-executive act without a thought of what he might be doing to the environment.'

'Your environment.'

Kirsten nodded emphatically. In the living-room, she walked backwards and forwards. 'I just don't know how to get him to appreciate my point of view. I've tried reason, persuasion, pleading, everything.'

'Everything?' Peter's question held innuendo and Kirsten, knowing what he meant, coloured involuntarily. 'Almost' was the true answer, but she did not give it.

'Aha!' remarked Peter knowingly.

'Not that,' she denied, but her words did not carry complete conviction.

'But almost.' Kirsten did not answer. There was a

dullness in Peter's voice that made her sad. If only he were the one who had the power to make her heart throb like a jungle drum!

'Cheer up.' He patted her shoulder. 'Things might not be as black as they look.' The back door opened and closed. 'Here's your chance to find out. See me to the door?'

They met Scott in the hall. He nodded distantly, but Kirsten wanted to challenge him there and then. By the time she had taken a breath to express her feelings, he had vanished up the stairs.

Peter bent to kiss her cheek and said he'd ring her some time. 'Thanks for the meal. One day I'll return the compliment, but it'll be my mum's cooking, not mine.' With a wave, he was on his way.

'Kirsten.' Scott was at the top of the stairs and she charged up them. He moved aside, eyebrows lifted as if he could not understand her aggression.

'How could you?' she attacked, trying to get her breath. 'How could you be so underhand about it all?'

'About "what all"?'

'Don't try to pretend you don't know!'

'OK, so I won't.' He strolled towards his room, removing his jacket as he went.

Kirsten followed him in, watching him discard the jacket and loosen his belt a notch. He must have eaten well, she thought jeeringly, probably anticipating the profit he would be making on the sale of Hazel Farm, not to mention the orchard. Yet his waistline was still narrow, with not a sign of surplus flesh.

Did he have to look so attractive, so lean yet solid, so supremely sure of himself? Did he adopt that attitude of self-assurance to daunt others, or was it basic to his personality? Both, I should imagine, Kirsten thought sourly. Well, he wouldn't daunt *her!*

Her hands found her hips and Scott's eyes swooped to them, appraising the outward curve they rested on, then lifted to the swell of her breasts as her white top tautened over them. So her physical shape attracted him? Well, she couldn't fight him with that, but she could with her mind, with her reason.

'How *could* you bring a property developer to the very edge of my garden, knowing how I feel about the whole subject?' Scott folded his arms, his jawline hardening as he listened. 'Not only will a housing estate look entirely out of place, it will bring down the value of Tall Trees.'

His eyebrows were two arrogant arcs. 'You're thinking of selling, after all? Name your price.'

'No, I'm not. You know what my intentions are.'

'Converting the house into retirement flats would affect the resale value, don't fool yourself about that.'

It might be true: Kirsten hadn't thought about it from that angle. 'Well . . .' She had to think of an answer to squash him! 'Maybe I've changed my mind. Maybe I'll spend the money I do manage to save making Tall Trees into the gracious residence it used to be, fit for a family——'

'Who's the lucky man?' His voice had the edge of a serrated knife. 'Count me out for the wedding reception.' He moved towards the door as if his intention was to show her out.

'I'm not getting married!' Her voice was shrill with annoyance and emphatic denial. 'There's no special man in my life.' There is, she thought, but he just doesn't want to know. Name of Scott Baird . . .

'So you've decided to live together.' His shoulders lifted. 'I'm broad-minded. I've done the same myself—in the past.'

Kirsten drew in her lips. 'You've got right away from

the point—deliberately! Which is, that you've secretly found a buyer for Hazel Farm, plus the orchard, for every bit of land, in fact, that borders on my property. Why haven't you been open about it?' she accused. 'Were you afraid to tell me?'

It must have been the jeering that fired Scott's fury. His hands clamped on to her upper arms. Then, as if he could not trust himself not to hurt her, he jerked away. Pivoting to the window, he stared outside, then turned, his anger conquered, if not vanquished.

'The man with me,' he said at last, 'was a landscape gardener. He was advising me about the resuscitation of the orchard. Yes, you might well look chastened. Especially as I've asked him to return some time and give me a quote for tackling your gardens—with your consent, of course.'

Full of contrition, Kirsten turned her anger in on itself. She pushed shakily at her hair, her eyes, wide with regret, meeting the blaze in his. 'I'm sorry, Scott.' She chewed her lower lip. 'And—and thanks. For your thoughtfulness, for everything.'

If she hoped he would approach and touch her—even, perhaps, kiss her?—she was disappointed. He merely nodded and watched for her next move, which was to retreat to the door. He did not stop her.

The door had almost closed behind her when she opened it again. He had not shifted. 'Peter and I—we're just friends, Scott. Truly, he's nothing more.'

'Even if he'd like to be?'

'He'd like to be.'

'But?'

With a tired smile, she nodded. 'But. On my side. Goodnight, Scott.'

His answer was to watch her leave, eyes enigmatic and deeply thoughtful.

For much of the following day, Kirsten caught only occasional glimpses of her tenant. He was wearing the most casual of clothes—she recognised the village shop's cotton shirt and denims—and he was working outside.

Hardly believing her eyes, she stood at the window and stared. Scott Baird, banker, wielder of money and power the world over, acting the builder's labourer and helping Fred Burns and Tommy!

Once she saw him trundling a wheelbarrow laden with bricks, his arm muscles echoing the strength of his thighs. Next time, he shovelled grey powder into the rumbling, rotating cement mixer, his body turning and twisting, revealing the build of an athlete rather than that of a desk-orientated city tycoon.

At lunchtime Kirsten sought him out. 'If you like,' she offered, 'I'll cook you a meal.'

Down on his haunches, the bunched muscles of his thighs tested to their limits the seams of the village store's denims.

'Thanks, but I'm going to the local,' he told her.

'Come with us, miss,' invited Fred Burns.

'Yeah, good idea,' Tommy backed him up. 'Nice to have some female company.' Like Scott, he plainly appreciated the femininity revealed by her blue T-shirt and neat matching skirt.

'No, thanks. I'll cook myself a——'

'Kirsten?' Scott rose, wiping his dusty palms on the seat of his jeans. 'You'd be welcome.'

'Well, I——' Her hesitation transmuted itself into a

nod. She hadn't really wanted to refuse, anyway.

Fred Burns took it for granted that Kirsten and Scott would want to sit together. He tugged Tommy from the windowseat just as he was lowering himself appreciatively beside Kirsten.

Scott arrived with the drinks, waving away all offers of payment. Smile mocking, he eased himself into the narrow space beside her. She wished he hadn't, then again, she was glad he had. Their shoulders pressed together. Their hips had no inhibitions about each other's nearness, while their adjacent thighs positively revelled in the way they ran parallel, indulging in a throbbing intimacy all their own.

While she read the menu, Kirsten darted little glances at the man beside her, glad that the menu card was large. To her embarrassment, Scott caught her looks, returning them with a burning stare of his own.

'Made up your mind yet, miss?' asked Tommy, plainly eager to make his choice.

As she nodded, Scott removed the card from her and, while the others studied it, moved his thigh fractionally nearer to hers, something that Kirsten had not thought possible.

Blushingly, she tried to discipline her reflexes, which to her dismay jumped in response to this man's every touch. She made to shift away, but the narrowness of the bench seat prevented it. Feeling her attempt to widen the space between them, Scott took the hand which lay on her lap and, using the table as a cover, put it palm down on his thigh. It was an intimate action which she remembered from the recent past, when he had looked after her during her illness.

The man's a positive lecher! she told herself,

endeavouring to work herself into a fury about him. Any woman would do, she was sure of that. But there was something inside her that would not listen to reason—a wild leap of desire that shook her as she felt the hardness of muscle and flesh beneath the hand Scott was pressing so relentlessly against him.

'Right,' said Mr Burns, 'I'll order the grub.'

'No,' Kirsten sprang up, desperate to escape from Scott's tactics, which were undermining her resolve to hold herself aloof, 'I'll get it.' She resisted the men's protestations and went to the bar, giving the order and staying there until the counter assistant told her it would take a few minutes to fulfil the order.

Reluctantly, she returned to her seat. The moment she squeezed in beside Scott he took her hand again, and this time held it openly and uninhibitedly.

'Aha, Kirsten could almost hear Fred thinking, I thought as much! Although what Tommy was thinking, she did not dare to guess. She took a sip of her drink while the others talked about the work they had accomplished and the jobs that remained.

'I'll be here for a day or two,' Scott told them. He glanced at Kirsten. 'You do know I'm Miss Ingram's tenant?'

And what more besides? Tommy's dour expression asked.

Fred nodded. 'It'll be a grand place, your Tall Trees, Miss Ingram,' he told her, 'when it's been weatherproofed and the alterations finished. A real country mansion, like.'

The food arrived and, as the men tucked into the crusty bread and hunks of cheese and pickle, Kirsten listened idly to their discussion. Enjoying the sharp taste of the pâté and the salad that accompanied it, she wondered at Scott's willingness to spend so much money restoring her property from which he, personally, would get little material, and no financial, return.

CHAPTER SEVEN

LATER that day, Kirsten was seated at her desk when Scott came to stand at her side. He still wore his working clothes.

Her hands stilled momentarily in their task of tidying up, her body tensing. She had found herself growing increasingly—and frighteningly—aware of him, and as he stood beside her now she wanted to rest her head sideways on his hip and tell him she loved him.

Instead she held herself rigid, asking touchily, 'What do you want?'

'You.'

Her head shot round and up. 'Don't be silly! We're not in the same league. Go back to the woman in your life—there must be one, a tall, handsome man like you.' She stared down at her desk. 'Let me guess. She's beautiful—of course—and slinky, and her taste in clothes is so out of this world, only the top designers can satisfy it. When you entertain, she's superb in the role of hostess; when you take her to bed, she knows exactly how to please you——Oh!'

Hands came at her, swinging her in the chair and dragging her out of it by the armpits. She was impelled against a chest like a rock-face and two lips took control of hers, proceeding to probe and explore until she was drained dry of defiance and resistance. They drew from her a response that made the blood pound in her ears and stole the breath from her lungs.

When Scott had finished with her, his taste-buds

109

finally satiated, she lay against him, staring helplessly into his eyes. Her mouth throbbed, her heart hammered and her arms lifted to link round his neck. But the telling gesture did not soften the line of his mouth.

'There was such a woman,' he said, his words clipped, 'as I told you, but she married my brother. Thank God she did, otherwise I would never have met you.'

Kirsten's head moved from side to side like that of a drunken person, and when she spoke, her words were slurred. Scott had intoxicated her with his kisses and already she was suffering from withdrawal symptoms. She wanted more of them, and more . . . 'What are you talking about, Scott? What difference has meeting me made to you?'

His eyes searched her face, lingering on each feature. His mouth was curved now and indulgent. 'You want me to put it into words? There's a better way.' His hand pressed on her rear and brought her against him. 'My God, can't you *feel*?'

'I can, I can,' she whispered, and warmth crept up, over her breasts and shoulders and face, darkening the brown of her eyes.

'I said I wanted you.'

Want, not love. 'I told you,' her cheek nuzzled his shoulder, 'I don't go in for affairs. I suppose I'm out of date, but that's the way it is, the way I'm made.'

'And I——'

'We're off, Mr Baird,' Fred Burns called from the kitchen. 'See you tomorrow, then?'

Cursing under his breath, Scott put her from him, striding in the direction of the caller. Kirsten held her face with shaking hands, wondering where her future lay; Scott's too. He couldn't stay there with this thing simmering between them, threatening at any moment to boil over in one gigantic, sizzling catastrophe. Because that was what it would be for her if she broke her own private vow to remain physically uninvolved until she met the right man . . . Her thoughts went in a circle. *Scott was the right man. Her heart was spilling over with love for him!*

So what am I waiting for? she chided herself. A proposal, a ring—wedding bells? Just how old-fashioned can I get? How——?

'Right, that's the builders sent on their way.' Scott leant against the doorframe, arms folded. He looked her over lazily, but she turned from him, afraid of giving herself away under such scrutiny. He lifted himself upright and approached slowly, and Kirsten tensed, not trusting her own reactions if he held her in his arms again.

Contrarily, she was disappointed when he walked past her and made for the boxes she had packed with the documents connected with the Hazelton-Baird estate.

Plainly, everything that had taken place between them before he'd been called away had been wiped clean from his mind. Had it all been so meaningless to him? Yes, she concluded, that was the truth, whether she was prepared to face it or not.

'I'll take these,' said Scott, lifting a couple of boxes. 'I'll be back for the others.'

Nodding, she busied herself with the papers on her desk, not turning when he collected the others. 'This all?' he asked.

'I've ransacked every drawer and cupboard. There's not a single bit of paper left that has anything remotely to do with your estate.'

His arm went across her shoulders, turning her. 'Thanks for the work you've done on it.' Kirsten studied the dust patches that clung to his working denims. He lifted her chin, brushing his thumb over her lips. 'It's no reflection on your ability or your integrity that I decided to bring in the professionals. There's a hell of a lot more work involved in my late great-uncle's estate than I realised at first glance. Unlike Lennard, I have no intention of letting the land lie fallow.'

Kirsten jerked away. 'Of course you haven't. You'll change everything, won't you? You'll interfere with people's lives, develop it and make it grow—upwards, not with wheat and barley, but bricks and mortar . . .'

Scott swung away and, collecting the remaining boxes, went upstairs again.

Kirsten was restless. The anniversary clock on the reproduction antique table downstairs chimed musically every hour. When two melodious notes told her it was the early hours of the next day, she threw back the covers.

Outside, the stars were twinkling pinpoints against a black velvet sky, while the three-quarter moon took the colour from the blossoms and gave them back a translucent silver.

She could not sleep. She told herself she might as well acknowledge the fact and read a few pages, but the book she wanted was downstairs. If she crept on tiptoe, she was sure she would not wake Scott. Pulling on a silky blue gown, she held her breath and opened the door. It swung soundlessly wide. The attempt at quietness was a pointless exercise.

Scott's door stood open, his lights full on. He sat on the bed, surrounded by papers and files. He saw Kirsten at once, his head lifting sharply, and he ran impatient fingers through his hair. His shirt was half unfastened and hanging loose, his dusty denims still in place. He was dark-jawed, his expression aggressive and faintly suspicious.

'What do you want?' he demanded.

'It's all right,' Kirsten declared, annoyed by his contentious attitude, 'I haven't come to seduce you. It's just that I can't sleep.'

'Sarcasm, my lovely,' he admonished, 'in the wee small hours, will get you nothing but trouble. If seduction's the name of the game, I can play at that too.'

He dusted his hands, rising and making as if to come towards her, head slightly lowered. Hurrying, she went on her way, calling over her shoulder, 'I'm going down for a book.'

Scott followed slowly, rubbing at the roughness of his jaw as he watched her searching on tables and chairs and even under cushions.

'Tried the library?' he queried drily. 'That's the usual place to find what you're looking for.'

'They're not my kind of books. They're Mr Hazelton's——' They weren't, they were hers now. But they weren't hers any more! She had never told Lennard Hazelton's great-nephew that she had disposed of the library, every single precious volume of it!

'Lennard left you the contents of the house. Which means those books belong to you.'

'Did, Scott. But not now.' The denial had come out of its own accord. She had not intended telling him yet, not at this unheard-of hour of the night, when they were both too tired to be pleasant.

'Not what?'

She muttered, continuing her search, 'It doesn't matter,' but he strode across the living-room, pulling her round. 'Not what?' he repeated.

Kirsten shook free, pulling tighter the sash of her dressing-gown. About to prevaricate again, her better judgement telling her to delay at least until morning the news of the sale, she saw Scott's determined expression. He would get it out of her somehow before the night was through.

'I needed the money.' She bent to shake up a cushion. 'I—I've disposed of the entire library.' There was no audible reaction, so she went on fidgeting with anything she could lay her hands on.

Putting a table and couch between them, she went on, 'I asked Mr Phipps for help. He said he knew a bookseller who might be interested—name of Stewartson, Oliver Stewartson.' She stole a glance, but his face was a closed book. 'I thought he might be interested only in the first editions, but he bought the lot. Had a client, he said, who wanted them.'

Finding the book she was looking for under a pile of magazines, she hugged it to her as if it were a bullet-proof shield. 'The money has been very useful to me, Scott.' She heard the note of appeal in her own voice, but she had every justification to be worried, hadn't she? After all, she guessed she should have offered them to Mr Hazelton's great-nephew first.

There was such a long pause, she looked at him, encountering no anger. A faint smile greeted her.

'I wondered when you were going to tell me.'

'You knew!' Relief transformed her face. Then doubts assailed her. 'Who told you the library was for sale? No, I can guess. Mr Phipps again.'

Scott inclined his head. 'And I asked Oliver Stewartson to come and put a valuation on the books.'

'*You* did?' Kirsten frowned. 'Why should you do that?'

'Maybe, like my great-uncle with Tall Trees, I wanted to keep them in the family? Some of those books have quite a value.'

'No wonder Mr Stewartson said the buyer wanted them to remain where they were for the time being! So,' she was still attempting to assimilate the news, 'I have you to thank for the money. It was a large sum, Scott.'

With his hands, he made a dismissive gesture.

'Even Peter thought the bookseller's client had paid over the odds.' A thought struck her. 'So why did you?'

'Why did I what? Offer in excess of the library's true value?' Scott hooked his thumbs over his belt. 'Now why did I do such an *unbusinesslike* thing?' His eyes swept her slender figure, from her tousled hair to the pink-painted toes pushing out of her fluffy mules.

'Your Mr Phipps told me a tale,' he went on, 'about this poverty-stricken young woman with a great old house on her back. She was desperately in need of cash to bring it back to a habitable level so that she could go on living in it. And wouldn't it be a pity, he said, to see his late old friend's valued books slip out of the family's possession?'

'So that was the real reason you bought them! Not for my benefit at all. Be honest.'

He moved stride by decisive stride towards her. 'It's inadvisable, Miss Ingram, at this dangerous hour of the night to tread on the toes of my temper.' He confronted her. 'You're determined, aren't you, at every opportunity, to downgrade and denigrate every effort I make to help you?'

'No, I'm not,' Kirsten answered a little wildly, 'I'm just searching through my mind for the truth. I can't see any possible reason why you should single me out for preferential treatment when there must be so many women in your life, you must be able to choose a different one for every day of the year, three hundred and sixty-five fabulous females . . . Don't!'

He had seized her shoulder and pulled her against

him, putting the hard line of his mouth to hers and working on it until it was forced to allow him access to the moistness it was trying so desperately to keep to itself. His other arm fastened like a steel hawser round her waist, impelling her to stillness and frustrating all her efforts to escape. Until she didn't want to escape any more.

When every inch of her yielding body told him that, even against her will, she would accede to his every whim, Scott relaxed his hold, but only sufficiently for his lips to move maddeningly against her ear.

'I did warn you, my own, not to kick my anger to life at this time of night.'

'I'm not your own!' snapped Kirsten, but it turned into a moan as his tongue made small circles round her ear. Breathless, fighting the desire that was weakening her limbs, she retaliated, 'I won't be number three hundred and sixty-six on your list!'

'How about being my number one on it?'

'I won't be that, either . . .' She tried to break free, but he easily restrained her. Staring at him, she asked, stupefied, 'What did you say?'

His arms firmed around her. 'I'm asking you,' he said softly, 'to be the only woman in my life. My wife.'

Her eyes, wide with incomprehension and fatigue, held his gaze. 'You're asking me to *marry* you? Yet just now you were warning me not to arouse your anger. It's the f-first time I've ever known a man propose marriage to a w-woman as a result of being angry with her!'

Scott lifted her chin and smiled down. 'Come on now, Kirsten, it was your words I was angry with, your insulting remarks about my private life. Not you.' His lips brushed hers, then he smoothed her hair, saying with a deep tenderness that almost melted her bones, 'Now, will you answer my question? Will you marry me?'

Was she, she wondered, in the middle of a dream, or was her tired brain inventing things that her rational, everyday mind would dismiss as pure fantasy?

Swaying, her body began to answer for her, her arms lifting to clasp round his neck, her eyes locking on to the deep warmth in his. 'Yes, oh yes, Scott,' she breathed, 'I would very much like to marry you. I love you, didn't you guess?'

For a passing moment his eyes hardened, then the flicker was gone and he was back with her. Had he looked into the past? 'There was a woman,' he had told her soon after she had met him. 'I offered her marriage, but she chose my brother. His bank balance was larger . . .'

'Darling Scott,' she whispered, 'I not only love you *now,* I'll keep on loving you for the rest of my life. I'll be loyal to you, I won't desert you, like your——' Ex-fiancée, she had been intending to add, but he was kissing her so breathtakingly the words were never spoken.

Even when the kiss was over, Scott continued to hold her. With her cheek against the rough hairs of his chest, she heard his heart pounding. Turning her lips, she kissed him where she thought those heartbeats were.

He groaned, resting his mouth against her head. 'You're straining my self-control to its limits, sweetheart. It's a dangerous time of night to tell a man you love him. Our barriers are down, for more reasons than one . . . unless——?' Cupping her face, he gazed into her eyes.

'Not yet, Scott. Do you mind? I have no way of——'

'OK, I understand. So we'll wait. But not for long,' he added with some force.

Eyes closed, Kirsten lay against him, still not

completely able to absorb the fundamental change of direction which had overtaken her life.

'I never believed,' she said, sighing with a deep contentment, 'that it was possible to be so happy.' Her head went back, her eyes tired yet alert. 'I don't know about you, darling, but I couldn't possibly relax enough to sleep yet. My thoughts are still jumping for joy!' Scott laughed, putting his lips to her temple. 'I feel like a soothing drink. How about you?'

'Fine by me. Except that I don't want to let you go.'

In the event, he did, following her into the kitchen. Straddling a stool, he watched her as she prepared the drinking chocolate, her filmy nightdress floating behind her.

'There you are, darling,' she said, placing the pottery mug in front of him on the scrubbed wooden table. He pulled up a stool for her and, side by side, they drank, his free hand holding hers.

Any moment, Kirsten thought, bemused, I'll wake up and find I've dreamt every wonderful moment of this night. Her hand tightened convulsively around Scott's. Just feel that, she told herself, this man beside me isn't just a dream, he's flesh and blood. He won't vanish with the coming of the dawn . . .

Feeling the greater pressure of her fingers, he lifted her hand, putting it to his lips and kissing it. 'I often go abroad. You know that?' he remarked, studying their linked hands. 'After our marriage, when my secretary books a seat for me, she can double it.'

Which showed, Kirsten thought, with a warm pleasure, how far his thoughts had pushed into the future, *their* future. 'I can go with you?' she asked.

'Four times out of five. Often there are receptions. Sometimes I give them for foreign dignitaries. In the past, my secretary's had a difficult job finding me a hostess.'

'Now I know why you want to marry me!' said Kirsten, laughing.

His head turned slowly. Lazy eyes moved over her and she realised how slender was the thread that held his self-control intact. 'Much more provocation, my lovely, and I'll *show* you why.'

He looked around the kitchen as if he were searching for something to distract his thoughts. 'That pile of magazines, are they the ones I gave you to look through? Right.' He thumped down his empty mug and, collecting the magazines, he led her into the living-room. 'Tell me what you've decided to buy.'

He dropped to the couch, pulling her down. His arm went round her and it seemed to Kirsten that it was the most natural thing in the world to be sitting beside her very new fiancé at nearly three in the morning, flicking through magazine pages and pointing to the items she had chosen.

'If it's going to cost too much, Scott, tell me and I'll——'

'Listen to this woman,' he broke in, ruffling her hair, 'worried about spending a man's money, and the one she's going to marry too! No one,' he added softly, 'could accuse *you* of worshipping the great god Mammon.'

Kirsten realised who Scott had had in mind—his ex-fiancée, now his brother's wife. Did that mean, she wondered hopefully, that on his woman-scale he had placed her, Kirsten, higher than the woman he had loved and lost?

Well, he's mine now, she told herself, and no one else's. I'm the one he's going to marry. Maybe, as time passed and she proved to him how enduring love—true love—could be, he would forget the woman who had made him so bitter about the opposite sex.

An all-enveloping yawn caught her unawares. Her head sank to his shoulder and her arms crept round him. The magazines flopped to the floor and her eyes closed. On the edge of sleep, she murmured, 'Sorry, darling. I'll go to bed.'

'Go to sleep,' Scott answered in a whisper. 'It's a much better idea.'

Arms enfolded her and she was lifted fully on to the couch. Only half aware now, she felt a hard male body shifting to make room, a living, breathing chest becoming her pillow. Warm, ardent lips were moving over her forehead, throat and mouth, and she lifted her lips to meet the kiss she most wanted. Then throwing off the tiredness, her body came alive. His hands had pushed aside the barrier of her nightdress, finding their way to her breasts, while his lips swiftly followed the trail they had blazed. But a profound shudder shook him as he put the brakes on their mutual desire.

'I want our child,' she heard him mutter against her throbbing flesh, 'to be born to both of us, not to you alone.'

'Yes, yes,' she whispered urgently, then she was folded into him and drifted into a dream. There was a cloud and she was floating on it. Scott was with her, telling her that of all the women in his life, he loved her the best, now and for ever more . . .

The anniversary clock pinged a delicate ten, awakening Kirsten with a start. Her hand felt for the man who had slept beside her from the small hours onward, but he had gone. A blanket had been thoughtfully placed over her and her mules lay neatly together on the carpet.

By the raised voices outside, she knew where Scott was now. There was the rumble of the cement mixer again. Boots stumped up the rungs of a ladder, while slates crashing to the ground elicited a robust curse that made her smile.

A carefree voice was raised in song, a little too near for comfort. Flustered, Kirsten tugged the blanket round her, pushed into the mules and made for the stairs. If she hurried, she might just avoid Tommy's inquisitive eyes peering through the glass doors.

Dropping on to her bed, she endeavoured to clear the mist from her thoughts. She had left this bed last night unattached and not too flush with money, returning to it now an engaged woman with a future free of monetary worries, having acquired a husband-to-be who not only meant more to her than anyone else in the world, but who had the financial power to give her whatever she asked for.

My name is Kirsten Ingram, she thought with a smile, otherwise known as Cinderella. It was a dream, it had to be! She loved Scott, and he loved her—he must do, she reasoned, since he had asked her to marry him. Surely nothing could happen to spoil their mutual happiness? Mutual? Well, she hoped so; hers, anyway. And, from the look on his face as he came into her room, Scott's too.

She pulled the blanket into place around her. 'What are you doing,' she asked with mock belligerence, 'behaving like an engaged man walking uninvited into your fiancée's bedroom?'

Scott eyed her lustily and she coloured, knowing she had asked for it. 'Don't provoke me,' he warned huskily. 'I can hardly keep these off you, as it is.' He held up his hands, then put them in his pockets. 'The other reason I'm here,' he went on, 'is because my own room's like an extension of my office. Except that my office has never been allowed by my secretary to resemble a scrap heap for lost letters and files. I didn't realise my great-uncle's affairs were so complicated.'

Taking advantage of her wonderful new relationship with him, Kirsten asked impudently, 'Sorry now you sacked me from my job as manager?'

'Not in the least. The more I go into it, the more I realise I should have lifted the whole business off your shoulders long ago. The moment I knew about my inheritance, in fact.'

'There you go again, doubting my managerial ability!' She jumped up and lifted a fist playfully in his face.

He grabbed it and opened his mouth wide, giving it a nip with flashing white teeth. As she yelped, he put it to his lips and kissed it, then pulled her to him. The blanket fell to the floor and he kicked it aside.

His arms twisted round her, his leg pushed between hers and through her thin nightgown she became aware of just how much she had aroused him. 'Darling, I——' She swallowed. 'Please, I——'

'Then don't entice me, witch.' Scott held her away and scanned her scantily attired figure. 'Look at you, flaunting your beauty at this time of the morning! If the builders weren't just outside and likely to call me at any moment, I'd——'

'Mr Baird!' It was Tommy from a discreet distance. 'Mr Burns says to tell you the plumber's come and will you tell him what you want done?'

Scott shouted in reply, started to release Kirsten, but changed his mind. His hands ran over her back and down to her hips, which he jerked against him. His kiss was fierce and possessive, then he strode from the room, leaving her gasping and wanting him back to make total love to her.

* * *

They all went to the Three White Horses again, Scott insisting that Kirsten accompany them. Quite openly, he held her hand, and the other two stared.

'You're the first to know,' Scott told the others. He looked deep into Kirsten's eyes. 'Miss Ingram and I are to be married.'

Fred Burns gave a shout of pleasure, then insisted on buying a round to toast the happy couple. Compliments flew and hands were shaken. Food was placed in front of Kirsten, but she ate only a little, excitement having stolen her appetite.

As Fred chewed a hunk of cheese, he commented thoughtfully, 'You won't want us to go on with our repairs and patching up, then, Mr Baird?'

Scott took a long drink before he answered, as if he needed time to consider the matter.

'Of course I want them to go on,' Kirsten put in quickly. 'Why should my engagement to Mr Baird alter my—our—plans?'

'Why, indeed!' remarked Scott, his eyes on his glass. It hadn't been a question, Kirsten noted, he had spoken reflectively.

Fred looked disconcerted. 'I thought Miss Ingram would be moving in with you after the wedding, that's all.'

Again Kirsten looked to Scott for help, and again he gave her none. Well, it was her house, wasn't it? And that meant he couldn't speak for her.

'He might be moving in with me, mightn't you, darling?'

He smiled. 'It's not impossible,' was his careful answer.

'This is early days, Mr Burns,' Kirsten pointed out. 'Our engagement is only a few hours old. We haven't discussed our future plans.'

'My fiancée's right, Fred,' said Scott at last. 'There's a lot to be talked about.'

'Fair enough.' Fred elbowed Tommy. 'So we carry on. Come on, lad, we've got work to do. This happy couple want some time to themselves.'

Once they were left alone, a silence descended. Kirsten wanted to slip her hand into Scott's, but something held her back. He seemed just a little aloof, out of her reach. She tried to bridge the gap.

'What are you thinking?' she asked with an attempt at playfulness, but he shook his head. Pushing away her half-empty plate, she commented with a wry smile, 'I seem to have lost the man I'm going to marry. There's a high-powered businessman come to sit beside me. I don't know him at all.' Scott smiled but made no comment.

Her mouth felt dry. It wasn't fear—she had absolutely nothing to be afraid of, had she? My name's Cinderella now, she reminded herself, smiling inside.

'It's true we have to talk,' he remarked at last. 'This idea of yours——'

'About converting Tall Trees into retirement flats?' she took him up eagerly. 'It can still go ahead. My marrying you will solve a lot of problems, in fact. The alterations can be carried out all the quicker, can't they? I'll come and live with you—won't I?' She frowned. She had so little knowledge of his personal life, she did not even know where his private residence was! 'Where do you live, Scott?'

'That's the point.' He leaned back and spread his arm along the bench seat. His fingers played with her hair and even that light touch started the melting process in her limbs. 'I lease an apartment in London. It's the only home I've got.'

Kirsten smiled, seizing his hand. 'Oh, you poor

homeless creature!' she teased. 'Worth a fortune, yet you've no place to call your own!'

'I,' he said, teeth clenched with mock menace, 'will make *you* my own before you're much older, madam. Come on,' he pulled her round the table, 'there are things we have to discuss.'

Hand in hand, they walked the mile back to Tall Trees. The sun had never shone so brightly, nor the birds' singing been more melodious. They entered the house through the kitchen and he took her in his arms. 'The wedding will have to be soon,' he muttered against her throat. 'Otherwise——'

Her hand, moing swiftly, covered his mouth. 'Are we going to have our talk now?'

'This evening. We're dining out, you and I. Meet me in the hall, seven-thirty. Right? I'll book a table at the Moated Castle.'

Peter rang that afternoon.

'Peter, hi!' exclaimed Kirsten, delighted to be able to tell him her news.

'What are you so happy about?' he asked. 'Someone else remembered you in his will?'

'Better than that. It's Scott and me. Peter, we're engaged! I'm so happy——'

There was a strangled pause. 'You don't mean it?'

'It's the truth, Peter. It only happened today.'

'Congratulations.' The word came dully, from stiff lips. 'So.' It sounded as if he was fiddling with the telephone cable. 'I never stood a chance, did I? I mean, with a tame millionaire around the place, you wouldn't look at a low-down architect.'

'I don't care a fig for his money,' Kirsten retorted.

'That's news. You went chasing after him for a loan, didn't you? And weren't you mad when you didn't get it? Maybe you agreed to marry him as the only way you knew of getting the cash you want out of him. Interest-free too. Marry a financial wizard and coax a fortune out of him, much better than a mere loan.'

It was his disappointment, Kirsten reasoned, that was making him so bitter. In her heart she forgave him, but she had to defend herself. 'It simply isn't true, and you know it. We love each other, and——' Well, she qualified to herself, I love Scott, even if he——

'OK, I can guess the rest.' There was a chopped-off sigh. 'It's just that—well, hope would keep springing eternal and all that. Hell, you know how it is, and . . . Cheers, Kirsten.' The phone crashed down.

Kirsten replaced her receiver more gently, as if it were Peter himself she was comforting.

CHAPTER EIGHT

A SCARLET candle stood on every table, each with its darting flame caught and mirrored by a silver holder. The *maître d'hôtel* showed them to a table for two.

'Will this suit you, sir?' he queried, pulling out a chair.

One flick of Scott's eyes told the man of his dissatisfaction. 'There must be a better one?'

With the trace of imperiousness to which Kirsten was growing accustomed, and which she reckoned came straight from his occupation of the prime position at boardroom tables around the world, he looked about him. 'Ah!' His eagle eye had identified the table that met his every need.

The *maître d'hôtel,* experienced in the ways of men who knew their own minds, had not taken offence. If anything, Kirsten noted with a smile, his respect for his fastidious client seemed to have increased.

'Certainly, sir—the table's yours. This way, madam, if you please.' A quick hand swooped to remove the reservation notice that was displayed on it. Someone else would have to accept second-best, Kirsten thought with a quiet smile.

Now they sat, side by side, in an alcove with a ruby-red lantern fixed to the wall above them, the flame of the candle flickering gently, the polished cutlery reflecting their own figures back at them. It picked up the blue and white zigzag pattern of Kirsten's off-the-shoulder dress as it flirted with the breadth of Scott's shoulders beneath his suit's impeccable cut.

Stealing a glance, she noted how his dark hair shone with life. She clasped her hands to resist the temptation of running a finger over the intractable line of his jaw. He was surveying the room, his sharp, evaluating appraisal telling her that, not far beneath the skin of the man beside her, was the business magnate and man of the city.

Idly, she wondered how his mind worked and was sure it would take a lifetime of marriage before she was able to work out its mysteries and complexities. Even then, much of it, she was sure, would remain an enigma.

Yet, when he shifted his gaze to rest on her, she felt herself melting helplessly in the warmth of his regard. This was the other side of him—the lover he would become, the virile husband he would one day be. And she felt that that day could not come too soon.

Impulsively, she put her hand on his thigh and he covered it at once with his. 'What was wrong,' she asked, glancing round, treasuring every moment of their time together, 'with the other table?'

'Too central, too conspicious. And I wanted to be near you. A man,' he took a sip from the drink he had brought from the bar, 'doesn't want to be a table's width away from the woman he's giving his ring to.'

He felt in his pocket and brought out a small, square box. Passing it to Kirsten, he smiled as she opened the lid, her eyes shining almost as brightly as the solitaire diamond the ring contained.

'If it doesn't fit, or if you don't like it, it can be changed or altered.'

'Like it? Oh, Scott, it's the most beautiful diamond I've ever seen! I'm half afraid to take it out.'

Scott reached across and extracted the ring, taking her left hand and slipping it on to her engagement finger. It was a perfect fit. Then he lifted her hand and put his lips to it. 'Welcome into my life, Kirsten Ingram,' he said softly, his eyes telling her a tale of wanting and desire.

With the flame of the candle dancing in her eyes, she whispered, 'I didn't realise until you came into mine, Scott, how empty *my* life was.'

A delicate clearing of the throat distracted them and, dropping her hand, Scott turned his attention to ordering the food and wine. It was in the course of the meal that he raised the question of possible wedding dates.

'It depends, doesn't it,' Kirsten queried with a smile, her side-glance catching the sparkle of the diamond, 'on the appointments in your diary? Don't tell me it doesn't, because I won't believe you.'

'Unfortunately, it does.' He took a sip of wine. 'I'll be returning to London in a day or two.' *I'll lose him!* The thought came inconsequentially and frighteningly out of the blue. 'If necessary,' he was saying, 'I'll rearrange some of them. I'm not waiting long, Kirsten.'

'I don't want us to, Scott,' she answered softly. 'More than anything in the world I want to be your wife.' She asked with some hesitancy, 'I suppose it couldn't be a quiet wedding, could it? I know it's a lot to ask a man in your position, but my parents have only just enough to live on——'

He looked at her, frowning. 'You must know that it won't cost them a penny, and that I intend to foot the bill? But, if you prefer us to marry quietly, then we'll have a quiet wedding.'

'Locally, Scott? I've lived in the area for some years, and I should love to be married here too.'

'Why not?' He looked about him. 'And this place will be fine for the reception.'

She wanted to hug him, but had to content herself with a peck on the cheek. 'You're being wonderful, Scott, and——' she shook her head '—I can't think why.'

'I'll tell you,' he murmured, 'when the time and the

place are right.'

They were seated side by side in the hotel lounge, coffee poured, when Scott remarked, 'I see there's a fairly sizeable income from my great-uncle Lennard's estate.'

'That's right. It comes from the various houses and cottages he owned, in and around the village. They're all in good repair. Mr Hazelton made it his business to keep them that way.'

'Good. As an engagement present, Kirsten,' he half turned to watch her face, 'I'm making over the rental from the entire estate to you.' At her gasp, he gripped her hand and added, 'In addition, after our marriage, I shall make you a personal allowance.'

She put her other hand over his which held hers. 'You're being so generous, I can't believe it! Darling, I——' She took a breath that turned into a sigh. 'If you're afraid I'll run off with another man with a bigger bank balance, like your ex . . .' Had she said too much?

'Like Lavinia.' It was, Kirsten realised, the first time he had mentioned her by name, and even then it had been spoken between gritted teeth. 'If you'd shown the least resemblance to her, I assure you I wouldn't have stepped across the threshold of your house that day.'

All the same, Kirsten thought with a twinge of unease, recalling the woman to mind, even speaking her name still had the power to provoke him to anger. How much did his proposal to her, Kirsten, have to do with his bitter rebound from the woman he had lost to his brother? Nothing at all, she told herself angrily—yet still the nagging doubt persisted that what was happening to her was too wonderful to be real . . .

The telephone rang as they stepped into the house. Kirsten snapped on the light and took the call. If it was Peter, asking permission to come . . . 'Scott,' she held out the telephone. His eyebrows lifted in query, and she told him, 'Your secretary. She said she's sorry it's so late, but she's been trying to get you all evening.'

He listened for a while, every inch now the business executive. In the dark suit he had donned for their celebration meal, he reminded Kirsten forcibly of the daunting tycoon she had encountered across the width of a desk the day she had gone to plead with him for a loan.

A sigh seemed to come from the depths of him. 'OK, tell him I'll bring my return forward. I'll be in tomorrow around ten. I'd planned a few more days here . . .' His eyes sought Kirsten's who was watching him nearby. He was listening again. 'Oh? What did *she* want?' His words were clipped, on the edge of anger.

At once Kirsten guessed the identity of the woman they were discussing, and her heart sank. By the taut note in his voice, she grew more certain than ever that, not only had Scott not freed himself from the influence of his former fiancée, but she in turn, it seemed, had not let him out of her life. But, a reasoned voice argued, she is his sister-in-law. It could be a family matter, couldn't it, that she was wanting to speak to him about?

'So she's pestering again,' Scott was saying. 'Tell her I'm not available, that my diary's full. Tell her——' his eyes swung again to Kirsten and this time they glittered with a kind of triumph '—I've been celebrating an engagement—mine. And tell her that from now on, until the wedding, which will be in a few weeks, I shall be completely occupied in my spare time. With Kirsten, my wife-to-be, of course. Thanks, Constance, for your good wishes.'

He rammed down the phone and held out his hand. Kirsten ran to him, putting hers into it and allowing herself to be swung into his arms. Of course he isn't using me as a shield, she told that irritating voice inside her head. A man of his calibre—needing a woman to hide behind, *from another woman*?

'That,' said Scott through drawn-back teeth, 'should cool her ardour.'

He put his mouth against Kirsten's and kissed her with a roughness that was, she was sure, a spin-off from his anger with his one-time fiancée. I hope, Kirsten thought, her head beginning to swim with the intensity of his embrace, he tells me all about her, gets her out of his system that way. If he can bring himself to talk about her dispassionately, it will mean that she really is part of his past.

When they separated, she looked up expectantly into his face, but although there was a light in his eyes she did not fool herself that it meant he loved her. It came, she told herself, forcing herself to face the truth, from their proximity, their intimate contact. His silence on the subject told her that he had put the woman called Lavinia to the back of his mind, not out of it, as she had so desperately hoped.

'I shall be gone a few days.' Scott tightened his hold on Kirsten's slim body as they stood in the living-room where they had had their late-night drinks.

'I intend to give an engagement party.' He kissed her lingeringly, savouring her taste. 'At my London apartment. Any objections?'

Her arms were loosely round his neck and their eyes went on making love. 'You're going to give me the country wedding I want: I agree to your engagement reception in the metropolis. Give and take, darling,' she whispered against the dark bristly shadow around his jawline, 'that's what they say marriage is all about.'

Outside her bedroom, they stopped, having climbed

the stairs linked together. 'I don't know how to thank you for your generosity,' she said, indicating the ring, 'for this and for the money from your estate.' Her eyes filled. 'I don't know how an ordinary girl like me managed to get herself a wonderful man like you. After all, all I've ever been in my working life is secretary to your great-uncle.'

'Stop fishing for compliments, Miss Ingram. You might get more than you bargained for. And I don't just mean compliments!' Scott's eyes lifted to survey her bed.

'I don't want to say "no", Scott, but——'

He pressed his fingers to her mouth and left her.

Showered and ready for bed, Kirsten stood at the window in the darkness. With all her heart she wished she had not sent Scott away. He understood her reason, she knew he did, and had agreed with it, but as she got into bed she was certain she would not sleep.

Counting sheep for the fourth time, she heard the door open. Scott clicked it shut and approached, his robe loosely tied, his hands in its pockets. There was a glimpse of chest hair, of bare thighs like muscled columns.

'Kirsten?' His voice was low and intense. 'I want my woman in my arms, not a million miles away.'

'Oh, darling,' she whispered, 'there's still a risk that——'

He bent over her. 'To hold you—no more, I swear. You can trust me, Kirsten.'

And she did, implicitly. She held out her arms and, as his robe dropped, she glimpsed his total maleness seconds before he came down beside her. As he entwined himself with her, she felt his arousal. Her heart throbbed in time with his, her breasts hardening at his nearness.

He slid down the narrow shoulder straps, putting his mouth to her warm breasts and stroking her responses to life. Then he found her mouth and kissed her to the brink of acquiescence.

'Scott, I——' she cried, drawing a choking breath. *I want you, I'm willing to take that risk,* she had so nearly told him. But he drew back, resting his moist forehead on her breasts, inhaling her scent, remaining there until he had regained control.

'Turn around,' he said at last, and she did so, away from him, fitting into the hard angles of him. His arms came round her and he held her with a sensual possession.

Surprisingly, she slept, and deeply too. In the night she stirred, scared for a few moments, until she remembered why she was not alone. She kissed the arm that still held her captive and snuggled back against him. He moved slightly, whispering her name, his mouth nuzzling the nape of her neck. But he put the brake on his desire and murmured that she should go to sleep again.

Waking to the distant pinging chimes of the clock—eight of them—she opened her eyes to find Scott bending over her, handsome in his dark suit and deep red tie. Here was the city executive again, the aura of the world of business around him already. The dusty man in clothes from the village store seemed to have vanished for ever.

Kirsten longed for that man to return. He was human and approachable. *He was very nearly her lover.* This man smiling down at her was heartless and dismissive, as she knew by painful experience.

'I'll call you, Kirsten,' he was saying huskily.

Her arms curled round his neck, her mouth rooting for his kiss. He put aside his executive briefcase and enfolded her in a deep embrace, penetrating her parted lips and telling her without words how much his body desired hers.

'I wish you didn't have to go.'

'How do you think I feel, having to tear myself away from this siren I'm engaged to?'

She kissed his mouth twice, then pushed him from her. 'Go now, darling,' she urged with a smile, 'before I entice you to your doom, like those sailors of old.'

He straightened, the blaze of desire in his eyes telling her what it was costing him to leave her.

Peter called in on his way home from work. He stood on the front step. 'Saw his lordship's car was missing.' He eyed her sourly, like a man on the trailing edge of a hangover. 'I take it I'm allowed to cross the threshold of the house owned by the wife-to-be of an international banker?'

Kirsten opened the door wider. 'Don't be an idiot, Peter. You know you're always welcome here.' He followed her into the kitchen. 'Why are you so bitter? I've never given you any encouragement about taking Robin's place.

'OK, so I had too much to drink last night. I went out with the crowd—someone got engaged. Great for them, bad news for me. I'd just lost the woman I wanted to another man.'

He sank into a chair and held his head. Kirsten looked at him with compassion. She liked him, he was the brother of her best friend, and that was exactly the feeling he aroused in her—sisterliness. If I told him that, she thought, he'd probably go out and get drunk all over again. 'I was just about to cook my evening meal. Want me to include you?'

He made a face, thought for a moment, then lifted a non-committal shoulder. She looked in the freezer.

'How about an asparagus quiche?'

Peter nodded dourly, but Kirsten noted that his eyes had brightened. In the event, he tucked in and, as his appetite was satisfied, so he grew more talkative.

'There's a rumour Hazel Farm's on the market.'

Kirsten went cold. 'It can't be true! Scott would have told me.'

'You kidding? He might be going to marry you—God, what a ring you're wearing!—but he's a businessman first and foremost. A guy rang the office. Said he might be interested in developing it residentially, and how were we placed for work if he wanted plans drawn up? Harry Bister—you know, the senior partner—said it'd be OK so long as it was some time in the future. At the moment, we had out hands full.'

Kirsten felt as though she wanted to cry. Some rumours were just that, without foundation, others were based on fact. Had Scott really let her down by offering the farm for sale behind her back, thinking he had occupied her mind sufficiently by filling it with excitement about their engagement?

She could not really believe it of him. Yet, as Peter said, his true world was finance. He was not made of the stuff that let the opportunity for adding to his fortune slip away for reasons of sentiment. Or for love. If that was what he felt towards her. He'd never actually said . . .

Having delivered his hand grenade—and consequently undermined his companion's touching belief in her beloved's integrity and selfless devotion—he volunteered to wash up, and whistled as he did so. As Kirsten dried and put the things away, the telephone rang.

Racing to answer it, she held her breath until the caller identified himself, then let it out on a long sigh of relief. Among other things, she could now challenge him about that rumour. But the man on the other end was definitely not the man who had left her with such reluctance that morning. He was the formidable creature across the desk, not quite ordering her from his august presence, but as near as a whisper to it. This was not the rich, warm voice of the would-be lover who had spent last night in her bed.

'How are you?' he asked, softening his voice a minuscule amount. 'Missed me?'

'Oh, Scott darling, it seems like days, not hours, since you left! When——?'

'I want you to come here, Kirsten. I'm going north for a couple of days, but three days' time? If you arrive at my apartment mid-afternoon, someone will let you in. I'll come as quickly as the traffic conditions allow. I've got a meeting in the morning and the party's at eight-thirty. All right with you?'

Kirsten felt dazed by the information that had been fed into her brain, each item in quick succession. 'Party? What party, Scott? Oh,' comprehension dawned, 'our party, our engagement.'

'Is the notice long enough for you to notify your friends?'

She considered the matter.

'I can't think of anyone I'd want to invite. It would be too far for my parents to make the journey. Marianne's abroad. There's Peter——'

'I said friends, Kirsten, not would-be boyfriends.'

The words had been quietly spoken, but they held a cutting edge that, had Kirsten ignored it, it would have been at her peril. She could have taken exception to the statement, become really angry, but she drew a steadying breath.

'I won't be bringing any guests, Scott, but thanks all the same. For the wedding, I'll invite the villagers, the people I know.'

'That's fine with me.' He gave her his address. 'I'll instruct the caterers to let you in. Then you can supervise their efforts, make any alterations you want. Feel free, Kirsten.' His tone had softened and her knees went a little weak. 'I'm missing you——'

At that moment Peter's whistle grew shriller, wafting out of the kitchen.

'Are you alone?' The softness had gone, the banker was back.

'Peter's here. He was a bit—well, a bit depressed, so I gave him a meal. Scott, there's a——' Instinct warned her not to question him about the rumour at that moment. It seemed the warning had been right, since he remained silent, ominously so.

'Peter's a friend, Scott,' she insisted, truly on the defensive now. 'And he's not staying the night, if it makes you any happier!'

She heard his slow breathing, as if he were controlling his reaction with an effort. 'I'll see you in three days, Kirsten.'

'Yes, Scott.' She paused. 'Book it in your desk diary, won't you?'

Staring at the silent telephone, she longed to call him back and tell him she was sorry for the sarcasm, but he had provoked her, after all, by doubting her loyalty to him . . . Her hand went out—then she realised she did not have his home telephone number, and his office had been closed hours ago. In the morning, he would be on his way north, out of touch, out of reach. How could she have been so thoughtless?

Peter appeared in the hall. 'Did he hear me?' he asked, his face wreathed in smiles.

Kirsten bit back the retort that sprang to her lips. He had just lifted himself out of his low spirits. She could not plunge him back into them, no matter how much dissension he might have caused, by his slightly sub-adult behaviour, between herself and the man she loved.

The caterers had left, promising to return in good time to set out the food, attend to the wines and arrange the bar. Kirsten looked around her, still in a state of semi-shock at the scale on which Scott seemed prepared to celebrate their engagement.

It was, she reflected a little wryly, because of the circles he moved in, his status in the world of business, not in deference to the social level of the girl he was marrying.

In the eyes of society, her parents were very ordinary people, her own standing simply that of one-time secretary to a man of medium wealth, her own status enhanced just a very small amount by the inheritance of his large house.

Wandering round, longing for Scott to come, she inhaled the heavy scents of the hothouse blooms the florists had provided. She admired the furnishings and décor of Scott's rented apartment and listened with surprise and awe to the distant roar of London's traffic which passed below, muted by the treble glazing built into the picture windows.

She still wore the clothes she had travelled in, leaving her suitcase in the small entrance lobby. She found Scott's bedroom, but without hesitation claimed the guest room, depositing her case in there.

Returning to his room, she stood at the window. Behind her was the wide bed, its dark blue covers matching the carpet and acting as a strong backdrop to the blue and cream floor-length curtains and drapery around the kidney-shaped dressing-table.

Her sigh expressed the restlessness inside her. When, staring out, she saw a man emerge from a car, slamming its door and feeding a parking meter, then throw his head back and look at her, her heart sang with joy.

Pausing to pull a comb—his comb—through her hair, she found she had misjudged the moment of his arrival. The key was in the lock and Scott was striding across the living-room and through the bedroom door.

Halting, he looked at her, his smile faint, his eyes glinting with expectation and just a little mockery. 'Caught you!' he said. 'Right place, right time.'

He peeled away his jacket and his shirt-sleeved arms came out like a blind man reaching for familiar territory. Kirsten went into those arms and they closed around her.

Reassurance came flooding back with the intoxication of his kisses, the caress of his hand as it penetrated the fastenings of her shirtwaister dress, cupping her breast as if it were the most precious thing in the world.

As a greeting, this was surpassing her expectations: the kind of coming together after parting which she had visualised in her dreams. Her hand ran over his face as if her fingers could not exist another second without palpable contact with those beloved contours.

His lips did the same to her features, memorising them one by one and leaving kisses imprinted there like a territory marker—*this woman belongs to me*.

'I want you, Kirsten. What's your answer?' he asked thickly.

'Darling,' her arms stretched over the span of his wide shoulders, 'there's nothing to stop us now, but—well, I have to shower and change——'

'So? We'll do that together.' Scott eased her dress from her shoulders, then cursed roundly as the doorbell chimed. 'Don't go away.' A few minutes later he returned, finding her in the living-area, dress in place again.

In his arms was a magnificent bouquet of flowers, which he passed to her. 'Read the card,' he suggested. 'They're not from me.'

' "To Kirsten," ' she read out, ' "to whom we give our beloved son for safe keeping. And for keeping him in order, too! Barbara and Graham Baird. PS We shall meet you at the wedding." '

Tears came into Kirsten's eyes. 'It's a wonderful gesture. They sound so nice, your parents. Show me where there's a vase, Scott.'

'Leave them,' he directed. 'The florists are coming back, they'll see to them. I've got my own particular hothouse bloom to wear in my buttonhole.'

With care, he took the cellophane-wrapped bouquet and placed it on a table. Then he held her again as if he could not bear his arms to be empty of her for more than a few minutes at a time.

'Not now.' The words came out with greater force than she had intended. 'Three days is a long time, Scott,' she tried to explain, 'when everything's so new, especially my fiancé.' She looked up at him with a touch of shyness. 'You're almost a stranger——' His mouth thinned and she rushed on, 'It's these surroundings. They do something to you——'

'For God's sake, Kirsten, you're romanticising! I'm a man, full of male wanting. It's overdue that I proved it to you,' he added grimly. 'I held back on the day of our engagement. It seems I was the fool. Is this your way of saying "thanks for your consideration"? To tell me I'm a *stranger*?' He had thrown aside his tie, unbuttoned his shirt. He seized her hand and put it palm first against his chest, holding her wrist in a vicelike grip.

Kirsten bit her lip at the bruising pain, but it did not make her want to draw away. Instead, she pushed her

other hand in too, then slid it round to the back of his
waist.

'That's better,' he said roughly, and wrapped his
arms about her, rocking her from side until her lips
reached up, parting and inviting the intrusion of his. He
took full advantage of her invitation, and when he
stopped she felt drunk and drugged at the same time,
wanting more of his kisses and yet more to satisfy her
need.

A distant church clock chiming from the heart of
London told them that the time of the party was nearer
than they had thought. Scott prised his mouth from hers
and swore softly, smiling down at her, his gaze both
possessive and anticipatory.

'Get changed,' he said huskily, releasing her with
reluctance.

'I'm using the guest room, Scott.'

'That'll do nicely,' he answered with a touch of
mockery, 'for the moment. But don't fool yourself into
thinking I'm intending to let my fiancée behave like a
guest when the crowd's gone home!'

He was ready before she was, entering without
knocking and resting back against the door, arms
folded. In his formal dress, his good looks were
devastating, the breadth of his shoulders pushing at the
generous cut of the jacket, his black hair still damp
from a shower.

Now he watched her through unreadable, appraising
eyes. She sent him a reproachful, embarrassed frown,
but he merely laughed.

'Get lost, she's telling me. Not on your life!'

Wanting to cover herself with something more than
her underwear, silky and attractive though it was,
Kirsten reached to the bed for her dress. Scott moved so
quickly that he was behind her and cupping her breasts

before she could move out of reach.

His mouth trailed stroking kisses over her bare shoulders and around her throat, and her head went back against him, her entire system trembling at the probing intimacy of his touch. Her skin prickled as his clothes brushed against it.

'Kiss me,' he demanded, hard fingers turning her head so that she was looking over her shoulder. Having no inclination to refuse, her mouth reached up, finding his lips waiting to be stimulated by hers. Plainly dissatisfied by her response, Scott spun her round and pressed her so far back under the force of his kiss that she was compelled to cling to him to prevent herself from falling.

Flushed and flustered, she pleaded with him to let her continue with her dressing. He surveyed her face, then reluctantly lifted her upright. 'Am I less of a *stranger* now?' he taunted.

No, she was thinking, as each minute passes, I'm discovering I don't really know you at all. She could not give voice to the thought because she knew it would provoke him so strongly, and she dared not think in what situation the first guests would find them as they started to arrive!

So she nodded, pulling on her dress and reaching round to fix the zip.

'Let me,' he insisted, taking her shoulder and slowly sliding the fastener into place. Then he stood behind her, admiring her reflection as she regarded herself in the mirror.

Part of her shoulders and all of her arms were bare, while the neckline dipped low at both back and front. Its colour, which was fuchsia, contrasted dramatically with the darkness of her hair. Its style, deceptively simple, yet with a clever cut, followed faithfully the outline of her shape.

She had seen it in the window of an exclusive little shop in the town. It looked stunning on her, the saleswoman had assured her, and now, seeing the gleam in Scott's reflected gaze, she had all the confirmation she needed that the woman's judgement had been right.

As she moved to the dressing-table to apply her make-up, he guessed her intention and reached for her. 'Before the colour goes on—quite unnecessarily, I might say—one more kiss.'

Kirsten sighed against him, her face turning to his like a flower to the sun.

'That,' he whispered against her cheek, 'will take me through part of the evening. Later, I'll need a booster, in a dark corner somewhere.'

She laughed and disentangled herself, but Scott did not go. He sat on the bed and watched as the cosmetics were applied, a faintly disapproving expression on his face, mingled with something like resignation over women's slightly ridiculous ways.

Finished at last, she stood up, and he looked her over. 'Touch me, touch me not, she's saying now. That damned make-up—if anything says "hands off", it's that!'

He raked in his pocket and produced a long, narrow jewellers' box. Prising open the lid, he extracted the contents—and Kirsten gasped. He took her wrist and slid his present on to it. 'An engagement gift,' he told her.

'Scott.' Her mouth had gone dry. It had been her dream to own a gold watch, but one with diamonds embedded around its casing? 'It—it must have cost a fortune! Oh, darling, I don't need gifts like this to make me love you. Haven't you guessed that by now? Besides, you've given me so much already.'

'It gives me pleasure to give them to you, believe me—to a woman who appreciates and values them, instead of——'

'Taking them for granted?' she broke in. 'Feeding her avarice and wanting more and more?'

'How did you guess?' His voice was heavy now, and sarcastic.

She put her arms round his neck and studied his face. 'Oh, Scott . . . You must have been hurt badly. I'll do my best to give you a better opinion of women.'

The doorbell chimed and he kissed her swiftly. 'Probably the caterers come back.'

While he was away, the bell rang again, reverberating over Scott's directives to the various helpers. They must have dispersed, since the noise died away. As Kirsten stepped into her shoes—in a colour to match her dress—the sound of voices reached her again, softer this time, intimate almost.

Icy fingers walked along her spine, as a jungle instinct deep inside scented a hidden threat. Her instinct for self-preservation was alerted as high-pitched feminine laughter registered on her extra-sensitive hearing. The first guest had arrived, and she knew by intuition and the prickling of her skin who that first guest was.

CHAPTER NINE

WHEN Lavinia Baird saw the young woman in the doorway, her eyes, flashing fire, swung to Scott. Entering the room, Kirsten reflected wryly that he must surely be heat-resistant to the core to have withstood the destructive force in that feline gaze!

'Well, well,' the woman drawled, moving sinuously towards Kirsten, 'if it isn't my beloved brother-in-law's beautiful new fiancée! Welcome, little Kirsten,' her white, perfectly manicured hand came out, 'to the Baird family.'

Little, Kirsten noted with a secret *moue,* which neatly reduces me in the eyes of the world—and most of all, Scott's. The 'handshake' was a mere touch, then a quick withdrawal from all contact.

'I hear,' purred Lavinia, 'that you were fortunate enough to inherit Lennard Hazelton's mansion. How wonderful for you, Miss Ingram!' You, a mere secretary, Kirsten interpreted, growing irritated by the woman's double-talk.

'Oh, please call me Kirsten,' she invited, with a deliberately cloying sweetness. 'After all, as you say, I am practically one of the family. Aren't I, darling?'

Moving to Scott's side, she slid her hand into his, then turned to face her husband-to-be's former wife-to-be. Her head high, confidence shone from every line and curve of her.

What the others did not know was that her hear was thudding with a primitive fear. This woman, her reason told her, might merely be a part of Scott's past, but intuition flashed warning signals—make no mistake about it, it said, this woman is your enemy and a threat to your future happiness with Scott: whatever you do, don't underestimate her power to destroy it.

'Darling,' with studied grace, Lavinia glided towards Scott, her clinging black dress highlighted dazzlingly by metallic blue sequins, 'I came to look over the arrangements. I foresaw,' her silky glance slid to Kirsten, 'that you might need my expert eye to spot any gaffes which a less—er——' her disdainful eyes skated over Kirsten's dress, but try as she might, she plainly found it difficult to fault her rival's appearance '—experienced person might miss.'

Scott looked down at the bright-faced woman by his side, his eyes carefully blank. 'Over to you, Kirsten,' he said, his smile softly mocking.

I'm sure he's enjoying this, Kirsten thought angrily. Well, Lavinia Baird is not going to be allowed to push me into any corner!

'I'm sure the *experts* Scott has employed to set up the party know exactly what they're doing, Mrs Baird,' she returned quietly. 'I'm also certain that they would resent any intrusion by a layman such as myself. Or you, of course.'

Lavinia's beautifully shaped lips withdrew into a thin, furious line. Her chin rose, her eyes hurled a look of disdain in Kirsten's direction, while the swinging movement of her willowy shape dismissed Scott's new fiancée as though she had ceased to exist.

'Larry's due here any moment, Scott darling,' she said. 'He wants a word in private. Something about a loan.' She smiled winningly into her brother-in-law's face. 'I told him that, knowing you as well as I do, I was certain you wouldn't let your sibling down in his hour of financial need.'

Knowing you as well as I do . . . Kirsten almost felt Lavinia's nails clawing her skin. The familiarity those words implied, the deliberate refusal to relinquish all possession!

Kirsten recalled Scott's cynical words when she had first met him. 'I offered a woman marriage. So did my elder brother, and he won. His bank balance was larger than mine.'

Now the 'winner' was after a loan—from the brother who had loved and lost. So whose bank balance was the larger nowadays? And which brother would the woman who, in the past, had opted for the richer of the two, choose now?

No, no, Kirsten thought fiercely, the 'choosing' is over. Scott's mine, and he's going to stay mine. There's nothing his ex-fiancée can do to part us, nothing at all . . .

The party was coming to an end. The guests had been drifting away for some time, although a handful lingered, latecomers, or those who were going on to a dinner date or a late show.

As Kirsten stood alone now, Scott's brother made his way towards her. A tall man, Larry Baird was as dark as Scott, but in his build he carried more flesh, his face and eyes empty of Scott's keen intelligence.

As he held up his glass in greeting, Larry's slightly glazed look told Kirsten he had already taken in more alcohol than his body could truly manage.

'Enjoyed the party?' His unsteady hand squeezed her arm.

'Very much, thanks.'

'Scott knows how to do these things. I'm not the social animal he is. But my wife is.' He watched them, his brother and Lavinia, as they laughed together across the room. 'Two of a kind,' Kirsten heard him mutter. 'A little bit on the side, that's what my wife likes. She thinks I don't know.' There was no missing the bitterness. 'Keep her out of his life, Kirsten.' Dull-eyed, he appraised her. 'You've got the looks, and I'm sure you've got the brains. But have you got the cunning to match hers?'

Flushing uncomfortably, Kirsten stared into her empty glass, telling herself that this was the talk of a half-intoxicated man. He didn't really know what he was saying, did he?

'I know why she married me,' he went on, 'and it wasn't for love—well, it was, but not of me. Of my money. She's never stopped wanting Scott. Now he's got money, she wants him even more. And what my wife wants, she usually gets. Anything in her way——' he made a wide, unsteady arc with his arm '—she sweeps it away.' He turned back as if he had just heard the words his lips had spoken. 'Sorry, dear. Forget all that, every nonsense word of it.'

He held up his glass again. 'Drink-talk, every bloody syllable! The man must love you, otherwise he wouldn't have proposed. Never again would he be fool enough to propose marriage to any woman, he told me when I married Lavinia instead of him walking her down the aisle. But he has.'

Larry started to walk away, then turned back, at the same time tossing the contents of his glass down his throat. 'Wouldn't give me a loan, the——' He mouthed the missing word. 'Not a penny, not a cent! Show some initiative first, brother, he told me, innovate, invent. In words of one syllable, come up with some new ideas.' He made a sound of disgust and walked falteringly away.

As he left her, his words worried at Kirsten's brain.

'Keep her out of his life,' Larry had told her. How am I supposed to do that? she wondered unhappily. Look at them now, look at Lavinia in Scott's arms . . .

They moved sensuously to the background music that still played. To Kirsten's eyes it was standstill dancing, calculated to provoke, to incite. Scott was near enough to inhale his ex-fiancée's perfume, feel her breath fanning his face, smile into her eyes . . .

Oh God, she thought desperately, has he *still* not got her out of his system?

The outer door closed. The last guest had gone and the caterers had left too. Tomorrow they would come, at Scott's special request, to clear away the post-party debris. Now there was silence.

'Kirsten.' One word, but it held command—telling her to turn round from the window and look at him.

He started to walk towards her, and Kirsten tensed. Did her blood have to flow faster with his every step? Did her heartbeats have to hammer so hard, almost deafening her, as his almost tangible magnetism cast its net and trapped her?

In a kind of defensive gesture, she turned to a beautiful flower arrangement, recognising the blooms as those which Scott's parents had sent her, their colours dazzling, their exotic scents filling her nostrils.

As she felt him brush against her, her breath came shallowly, but something stubborn inside her would not let her do as he wanted. Instead she moved along, tidying the discarded bottles and decanters, her movements jerky.

Two glasses were firmly removed from her gripping fingers. Hard hands turned her to face a faintly mocking smile. 'Society hostesses don't do their own clearing away.' Scott's tone was indulgent, but his eyes carried a trace of anger at her faintly hostile attitude.

Well, she decided, she would show him that she could get angry too! Hadn't it been obvious to everyone present that, although the party had been given to celebrate his engagement to the woman he had chosen to be his wife, his sister-in-law still had an unmistakable hold over his sensual inclinations?

For much of the evening, and under cover of her kinship with him through his brother, she had made an undisguised play of claiming him as hers. So what if there had been others around them? Lavinia's arm had slid, ostentatiously—and worse, *unrepelled,* through his.

'Don't they?' Kirsten replied, answering his statement. 'Ah, now, that's where you're wrong.' Her brown eyes challenged the amber of his. '*This* one does,' indicating herself, 'but then, you see, I'm not really a "society" hostess, just one of the ordinary, humdrum variety. Want to trade me in for a more suitable model?'

Scott's narrowed gaze told her he knew to whom she was referring.

'One much more appropriate to your status in life,' she went on recklessly, 'made to measure, in fact, super-glamorous, gift-wrapped in gold leaf?'

'What the hell are you talking about?' he demanded roughly. 'What's sparked off this spate of sarcasm?' Realisation dawned. 'I saw Larry talking to you. What did he say? No, I can guess. He always did try and blame others for his own shortcomings.'

The telephone rang and he cursed roundly, staring at the instrument across the room. 'Go to——' he growled, but changed his mind and answered it.

'Yes? *Larry?* For God's sake, man, did you really think I'd talk business at this time of night? Have a heart! Mr fiancée's waiting . . .' His eyes swept in a circle round her like the embrace his arms seemed to want to give. 'She persuaded you to ring?'

It seemed that the telephone at the other end changed hands, and a softly spoken feminine voice crept into the room. It sent shivers down Kirsten's spine. A disconsolate slope to her shoulders, she stood at the window. Her bare arms prickled in the dark breeze, her unseeing gaze sweeping over the brilliant, restless lights of London.

So, she agonised, how am I supposed to keep Scott's one-time lover out of his life when, according to her husband—and this clever, slyly timed telephone conversation proves he's right—she possesses cunning, along with all her other feminine assets?

Scott's conversation with Lavinia continued for some time. From the phrases Kirsten picked up, she guessed it was about business—but with a very special client. Scott's subtle tone-change told her without any doubt that his approach to his one-time fiancée was not the one that was usually adopted by banker to would-be customer. Where now was the tough, inflexible business man who had so brusquely refused a loan to her?

Aren't I justified, she asked herself, in feeling resentment? Then fear crept in as once again it became clear that, deep down, Scott had not broken completely free of his ex-fiancée's influence. After all, she reminded herself, it was Lavinia who had broken off the relationship, not Scott.

There was no doubt about it, his 'goodbye' to his sister-in-law held more consideration and tolerance than if he had been speaking to his brother. Hearing him approach as if nothing had happened. Kirsten felt something snap inside her. She swung round.

'Why don't you go back to her?' she stormed. 'She's never stopped wanting you, or so her husband says.'

Scott's mouth tightened. 'My brother Larry's done his work well, hasn't he? Sown his seeds of doubt, and made sure they've taken root.'

'How do I know whether you've ever stopped wanting *her*? Judging by the way you were running at her call this evening . . .'

Anger flashed in his eyes and a muscle worked ominously in his cheek. 'So she still wants me, does she? But she won't get. She made her choice—and I've made mine. And for your information,' the thrust of his jaw told Kirsten she had found the hard core of him, 'I stopped wanting her long before the moment I started wanting you. Now, I think it's time,' he reached out and jerked her against him, 'my "wanting" was appeased. And your *jealousy* set at rest—in my bed, and in my arms.'

Kirsten made to struggle, but his arms were like iron, stilling her easily. 'If you think that making love to me will make me forget my doubts——'

'I don't just "think", I *know*. And not just your doubts. You'll forget everything but the two of us. Didn't you discover that in your former lover's arms?'

'I *told* you—Robin wasn't my lover.' Her flushed face still defied him. 'And who's the jealous one now?'

'You think I'm jealous of your ex-boyfriend? With the emphasis on *boy*.' Scott's fingertips skimmed down her arms, leaving a tingling trail. 'I'll show you, Kirsten, how a *man* makes love. How old was he—your age? I can give him eight years. I'll demonstrate to you how maturity can deepen experience. Yours and mine. My God,' he ran his hand over her shape, 'how I've longed to touch you! All evening I've thought about how you feel in my arms, how in this beautiful body of yours,' his voice was softer now, 'you encapsulate heaven for me. Yet all that time you thought I was *running at*

Lavinia's call? It was you who called the tune, Kirsten, every minute of every endless hour that passed.'

He swung her into his arms and pushed with his shoulder at his bedroom door. As he lowered her to her feet, her shoes slipped off. His hand found the zip fastener which, a few hours earlier, he had pulled up, sliding it down now with a sure hand and slipping the neckline from her shoulders. Then the dress lay in a heap at her feet and he lifted her free of it.

His palms smoothed their way over her bare shoulders, lowering the straps of the bra until it unhooked of its own accord. He tossed it away and his mouth made a circle round each nipple, drawing her throbbing flesh inwards between his teeth, teasing each one until she cried out and pressed her fingers into the sinewy muscles of his arms.

As she stood naked before him he held her at arm's length, stroking her with his eyes. 'If Robin wasn't your lover, then who was?' he asked thickly.

'There's been no one, Scott. Not until the right man, I decided. So I'm old-fashioned . . .' Her smooth shoulder lifted and he put his lips to it.

'And I'm the right man?'

Mutely she nodded, a movement that was tantamount to giving herself into his keeping.

His eyebrows lifted, his mouth curved in a faint smile and Kirsten guessed he was pleased. 'These days, what a find my fiancée is,' he said softly. 'So you're presenting me with pastures new, untrodden by any man?' His palms ran over her, resting on her heart and smiling as the drumming beat pulsed against his palm. 'You're so beautiful, Kirsten—you probably don't know how beautiful. Your face, your body . . . God, I want you!' He pulled her against him. 'I'm crazy for you. Undress me,' he murmured.

He helped as her shy fingers wrestled with buttons. At his waistband he took over, finishing the job. She rejoiced in the sinew and muscle of his nakedness, the breadth of his shoulders beneath her stroking hands. Then, when he brought her close, she felt his taut, hard thighs, the rough hair of his leg rasping against the softness of her inner thighs as he pushed it between them. Most of all, there was the exciting, thrusting maleness of him.

As they lay together on his bed, her body twisted and lifted, her parched mouth opening on a soundless cry as Scott's hands sought out and probed her secret places. Joyfully she responded to the sheer male strength of him as he brought her to the pinnacle of need, her whole being crying out for his possession.

'Take me now,' she heard herself plead, and drew in a shuddering breath as he entered into her. She lost all sense of time and place as reality receded and a dreamlike sensation lifted her, with him, to a shattering climax. Mouth on mouth, they stayed there, bodies entwined, golden sunlight playing over their eyes even though the moon claimed the sun's place in the sky.

With the first hint of daylight, Scott took her again, his lovemaking more leisurely this time, drawing out each caress and intimate invasion before his body possessed hers once more.

Waking again, Kirsten heard his deep breathing, found his arm cradling her breasts, his drawn-up leg linking itself to her thigh. Birdsong joined the music in her mind and the sun's golden rays, trapped outside by the curtains, called her to the window to let them in.

Easing herself from Scott's embrace, she pulled on a black silk kimono which she found hanging on the door. Being Scott's, it was large enough to encircle her slender body twice. She tiptoed to the window, drawing back the curtains and gazing out.

She felt both contentment and elation, her body passing messages to her brain that life was wonderful and all the world should share her joy.

Her gaze spread out across the great park that stretched away from the wide, impersonal streets already busy with traffic. Then her thoughts returned to Tall Trees, where birdsong filled the air from daybreak until dusk with no build-up of traffic noise to drown it, where the garden's riot of colour crept through the windows and became part of the décor of the house.

'What are you thinking?' Scott, speaking close behind her, made her jump. His arms wrapped round her, slipping beneath the loosely hanging kimono and stroking her softly throbbing flesh.

He was arousing her again, and her breath shortened, causing her throat to jerk out the answer. 'About my home.'

'Ours when we're married?'

She nodded.

'Will you let me into it? Not just physically, but in your mind?'

'In other words, share it with you?' She turned within his arms and he eased away the covering she had pulled on, his hands tracing her shape and filling her with a shivering desire. 'Just having you there, Scott,' she whispered, 'will deepen my pleasure in it.' Her fingertip rubbed over the rough morning shadow around his cheeks and jaw. 'I mean it.'

'Thanks for that, my love.' He tipped her face and kissed her eyes one by one, moving to her mouth and touching down in soft, erotic landings. Then he pulled her close, and groaned, burying his face in her neck and inhaling her perfume. 'I want you again, sweetheart.

Later, I must leave you and get back to work. For a few hours, no more.' His burning gaze appraised her. 'That's about as long as I can stand away from you.'

'My love', he'd called her, she noted with pleasure as he lifted her back to bed. Which, she thought as soberly as the circumstances would allow, did not mean he meant it, nor that he loved her, but it would do, wouldn't it, to be going on with? She would have to content herself with that.

Scott had left her behind reluctantly. 'Tonight I'll take you dining and dancing,' he had promised. 'We'll spend the weekend going places. Or staying right here.'

'Here, do you mean?' Laughing, she had thumped the bed, sitting on it in his black kimono.

'Can you think of a better place?' he had joked, but that look in his eyes had been serious.

Kirsten had seen him out of the apartment, hands straightening his tie. There was something she wanted to ask him. She had been putting it off, but she couldn't wait until his return that evening.

'Will you tell me something, Scott?' He'd put down his executive case and linked his arms loosely round her waist. 'There's been a rumour going round in the village—it says that you've sold Hazel Farm. Will you tell me if it's true?'

The question was out and she'd dared not raise her eyes above the knot in his tie. He hadn't removed his hands, but she'd been sure he'd removed part of himself from her.

'I have not sold Hazel Farm.' He had bent to retrieve his case and his eyes, as he'd straightened, had been impersonal. 'Anything else you want to know?'

Yes, a voice inside her had cried out, do you love me? But she had shaken her head. Something about the way she'd turned away must have touched him. He had dropped the case and taken her in his arms.

Her finger had stroked a path beneath his eyes. 'They're warm again. Just now, they almost froze me out!'

Laughing, Scott had pulled her to him, kissing her breath away. She'd clung, not wanting him to go. Now, showered and dressed, she cleared away the dishes left over from the breakfast they had shared.

The caterers arrived, and in less than a hour the apartment was back to normal. Wandering to the window, Kirsten wondered what to do with the time that stretched ahead until Scott returned.

The telephone rang and she flew to answer it. It was Scott, and she could almost see his face lighting up, asking how she was.

'I'm missing you a lot, darling,' she told him. 'I'm counting the minutes until you——'

'Kirsten, it's a bloody nuisance, but I've had an urgent summons from one of our branches abroad— Switzerland, in fact. I'm off there on the first available flight. I keep all the necessaries here for emergencies like this.' He must have heard her jerking sigh. 'My love, I'm as annoyed as you are.'

'How long for, Scott?'

'A week, I hope no more. Stay right there until I get back. Sleep in my bed, Kirsten. Then I can visualise you . . .'

It took her some time to come to terms with her bitter disappointment. When the doorbell rang, she dared to ask, heart racing, had he come to say goodbye?

A voice announced imperiously over the entryphone, 'This is Lavinia Baird. I have a key, but discretion suggested I should ring. Will you let me in, please?'

Lavinia's eyes talked first, telling her hostess just how

much of a country girl she looked, in her white cotton shirt and pale blue trousers.

'I'm sorry,' said Kirsten with a cool politeness, 'but Scott's at work.'

'I know all his movements,' Lavinia remarked, sweeping into the living-area, her perfume leaving an exotic trail.

'Naturally. You are his sister-in-law, after all.'

'And his former lover. Never forget that.'

Does she think she can get the better of me? Kirsten thought furiously. 'Discarded mistress, don't you mean?'

The green eyes smoked darkly, then cleared. Lavinia's smile was that of a woman who held the trump card. In her expensive, softly tailored, grey check suit, the tie of the white blouse secured with a ruby and pearl brooch, she looked every inch the banker's wife—which she was not.

If her husband, Larry, needed a loan so desperately, Kirsten reasoned, then who was the provider of the money that paid for the exquisite clothes and jewellery Lavinia wore? Or was she the cause of her husband's financial embarrassment?

Lavinia wandered round, then made for Scott's bedroom, plainly knowing the way blindfold. Her eagle-sharp eyes noted the disarray which Kirsten had not yet got around to tidying, the kimono on the floor, the dishevelled bedclothes telling their own tale.

There was a flash like forked lightning as Lavinia flicked her regard back to Kirsten. 'So you've really got him!' The words came out like a snake's hiss. 'I suppose you think you've won?'

So it was to be open warfare, no feigned politeness, no holds barred? Kirsten pretended naïvety, asking, 'Won what, Mrs Baird?'

'Luxurious living, inexhaustible wealth. *Scott!*' Her glance bounced off the watch that sparkled on Kirsten's wrist. 'Fabulous jewellery, priceless gifts.' Her lip curled. 'A man's token of gratitude to his lover of the moment, Miss Ingram, *not a token of love.*'

Was the woman so clever, Kirsten wondered, reeling inwardly, that she could spot a rival's weakness, then play on her innermost doubts? How often had she, Kirsten, longed to ask Scott if he loved her? Did a man ever call a woman 'my love', if he didn't? But the answer was clear, surely? If, at the time, he was making love to her, of course he would call her 'his love'.

Kirsten walked across to Scott's bedroom door, closing it firmly. What goes on in there from now on, the action declared, is Scott's—and my—business.

'So, how can I help you?' she asked, her smile telling her adversary that once, she might have had the run, and the running, of Scott's flat, but now it was Kirsten who was in charge.

Lavinia sank gracefully into a chair, draping her arms along the chair's upholstery, her gold bracelets chinking. 'It's the other way round, Miss Ingram,' she drawled. 'It's I who can help you. For instance, I can tell you why Scott is intending to marry you.'

'Because he loves me,' Kirsten riposted with a bravado she did not feel.

'My, you *have* fooled yourself, haven't you? Or has he been cleverer than I thought?' Lavinia jumped to her feet. 'He wants your house, that's why. For building purposes,' she added with a snarl.

Kirsten's legs almost gave way. 'You're talking nonsense,' she managed. But was she? she thought in anguish. Hadn't Scott offered her money for Tall Trees, increasing the amount each time she had refused? Hadn't he offered to repair the place; asked to rent some rooms—*thus getting his foot in the door, then himself through it.*

Then he had proposed marriage, which meant that after the wedding he would have had unlimited access to the place. Then, her thoughts sped on, through coaxing and lovemaking, he would at last persuade her to hand the house over to him. *After which, he would proceed to demolish it . . .*

'I don't believe you.' The words were defiant, but her fire had died. 'Where did you get your information?'

Recognising signs of defeat, Lavinia smiled triumphantly. 'Scott's great-uncle's letter, written for him to read after the man's death.'

In no way could Kirsten doubt the existence of such a letter. Mr Phipps had waved it before her eyes the day he had informed her of her inheritance. 'It's addressed to a Mr Scott Baird,' Mr Phipps had disclosed. 'Strictly private . . . living in London . . .'

'What about that letter?' Her voice was fainter now.

'I saw what it contained.'

'Scott showed it to you?'

Lavinia gave an amused nod. 'There were instructions. Well, let's say, advice.' She patted the tie of her blouse, reassuring herself that the brooch was firmly fastened. 'It was short and to the point. It said—I can remember the exact words—"If you want the house, you'll have to marry the girl." '

Kirsten swung to the window. She wanted to scream at the top of her voice, you're lying! But she couldn't. She knew so well the late Lennard Hazelton's quixotic ways. Hadn't they been demonstrated only too plainly—with a final flourish—in the way he had left Tall Trees to his secretary, yet had passed the estate encircling it to his great-nephew?

Lavinia took her leave, having watched with unconcealed satisfaction the collapse of her opponent's confidence, the melting away of her aura of radiance into uncertainty and doubt.

Kirsten was left staring reality in the face. Even if she picked up the phone and demanded the truth, she wouldn't get it. Of course Scott would deny Lavinia's allegation—with indignation and with anger; she knew him well enough now to judge his reaction in advance. And of course he would insist he loved her, wanting to marry her for that reason, and that alone. *He wanted the house, didn't he?*

It took her only a few minutes to pack. Plunging into the noise and rush of London, she felt too numb for tears. People ebbed and flowed around her. She was back in the river of everyday life and the temperature was cold indeed. The current was strong, it was dragging her down, and she was drowning . . .

Kirsten rang Cherry Marston. 'Will you come tomorrow as usual? I'm home again.'

'Is the gentleman with you, Miss Ingram? How was the engagement party? Did you have a good time?'

'It was fine, thanks,' Kirsten answered, twisting Scott's diamond ring which she still wore, having left only the watch benind.

For the present, she had decided, it would be simpler to pretend that nothing had changed; easier, her thinking went, to explain a slow drifting apart than a sudden break. 'Mr Baird's not with me, Cherry. He was called abroad unexpectedly.' That part was true, Kirsten thought. 'So I came back.'

Peter rang that evening. 'The grapevine tells me you're home—alone. Can I come over? My parents have gone for a month's cruise around the Carribean, so

I'm feeling lonesome.'

'Tomorrow, Peter, if you like.' That would give her a few more hours to adjust to the idea of living without Scott for the rest of her life. Adjust, maybe, but never would she be able to reconcile herself to it. The feeling of let-down, after the golden dream of a lifetime with Scott beside her, underscored her every action and thought.

It was his hypocrisy which she found hardest of all to forgive. If only he had come right out with it—asked her to become his wife so that her inheritance would become his and Tall Trees slip unnoticed and unopposed into his possession—then she might at least have felt some respect for his honesty.

'I'm on a surveying job tomorrow afternoon,' Peter told her, 'way out in the country. When I've finished, I'll call in for—er—a chat?'

Kirsten had to smile. 'Don't you mean for a meal? OK, I'll look forward to seeing you. Or should I say, to feeding you?'

Fred Burns and Tommy had cheerfully recommenced their work. Kirsten did not enjoy telling them that, after today, she wanted them to suspend their activities for the time being.

'Change of plan,' she added succinctly, and did not elaborate, despite Mr Burns' raised eyebrows and Tommy's surprised whistle.

It was just after her lunch break that the telephone rang. This was the moment she had been dreading. Half inclined to ignore the instrument's demand to be answered, she lifted the handpiece and listened, saying nothing.

'Miss—er—Ingram? Is that Miss Kirsten Ingram? We've been given your number by——' Here, the caller waited for a response.

'Speaking.' Her heartbeats were going like a drum, but the woman at the other end did not sound like a secretary.

'This is Featherstone Hospital, Miss Ingram. We have a Mr Peter Harvey in our care. His parents and sister are out of the country and he's given us your name——'

'Oh, please, tell me—has something happened?' Peter was not the man of her choice, but he was a friend, a rather dear one.

'He had an accident, damaged his car. That's been taken care of. He's injured his legs, one more than the other.' The woman explained in greater detail, but Kirsten could not take in the medical aspect. 'Broken bones in one foot, bruised ligaments. He can't be left alone at present, Miss Ingram. He says you'd have room to take him in, if you'd agree. Doesn't want to impose, he says——'

'Of course he must come here. Do you want me to collect him?'

'The ambulance will be bringing him to you in about one hour. Thank you for your help, Miss Ingram.' The woman rang off.

By the time the ambulance arrived, there was a sofa bed made up in the room that had always been designated the parlour. Food was sizzling in the oven for their shared evening meal.

When the ambulance team wheeled Peter into the house, Kirsten was relieved beyond words to see his wide if rueful grin, pointing thumbs down to the plaster which encased one of his legs. The other, while looking normal, was in fact bandaged and only fractionally more mobile.

Sprawled in a chair, Peter sighed, shock threatening to surface. Drinking tea which Kirsten had made, he said, 'It looks worse than it really is. I suppose you could say I was lucky.'

Kirsten made a face at his legs. 'Call that lucky?'

'I certainly do. I told you my appointment was out in the country? You know how narrow those roads are—well, this one certainly wasn't made for lorries coming head-on! This guy was driving so fast, I knew he couldn't stop in time, so I swerved to avoid him. The car went down the verge, then rolled over into a field.'

Kirsten winced.

'So—lucky me. Sorry to land myself on you, Kirsten, but there's no one else to turn to at the moment. You'll have to explain to macho Baird that I've got no evil intentions towards his beloved——'

'It's over. I walked out.' She paused, wondering how much to tell. 'I—well, I discovered why he wanted to marry me. And it wasn't for love.' Peter was waiting, his manner gentle. 'It was for my inheritance.'

'This house? Did he tell you?'

'Someone else did.'

'Reliable source?'

She let out a sigh. 'Impeccable—his sister-in-law. So, it's over.'

'Does he know? No?' He let out a tuneless whistle. 'Expect the skies to fall when he does. In my judgement, he's not a man to be trifled with.'

'I can raise a storm any time I need to. He's not the only one.' Kirsten's lip started to tremble and she turned away sharply towards the kitchen. Returning, she asked, 'Just how mobile are you? And self-sufficient?'

Peter laughed. 'If you mean, do I need a nursemaid and a nanny, the answer's no. Think I'd let you into my really private life? Not on your——' The telephone rang.

Kirsten stood stiffly in shock.

'Sock it to him, pal,' murmured Peter, sweeping with his arm towards the hallway.

'What the hell,' the voice through the receiver demanded, 'are you doing at home? I tried all yesterday, now all day today to get through to you. For God's sake, Kirsten——'

'You don't ever need to worry about me again.'

There was a silence that seemed endless, probably about five seconds, Kirsten reckoned. Her heartbeats were rat-tatting like a machine-gun. 'What are you talking about?' The words were clipped, coolly polite, cutting into her more deeply than sarcasm.

I've discovered your guilty secret. You wanted my house, not me. The accusing words were there, rattling around in her brain, but she wouldn't let them out. Scott would only deny it, tell her he loved her, that she was the only woman . . . and so on, when she knew for certain that it would all be lies.

'I decided,' she said, speaking clearly, 'that I couldn't take your life-style, that's all.'

'*That's all?*' His voice was coated with ice, and her teeth began to chatter silently with reaction.

'That's all,' she responded, commending herself on her steady, chilling tone. 'I haven't found myself a man with a bigger bank balance, like the other woman you proposed to.' She heard the hiss of his indrawn breath, knew she had hurt him, but was beyond caring. 'I just wanted out, like a pet cat that needs to revert to its wild primitive state and roam the countryside now and then.'

There was a bellow of laughter from the living-room, and Kirsten closed her eyes in despair. But maybe Scott hadn't heard?

'Now tell me the truth,' he snarled. 'You couldn't get the boyfriend out of your mind. And I don't mean the ex, I mean the one who took his place. Now you've been initiated into the art of love, you're raring to go with another man. So do your roaming, flex your claws. I'm finished with women—and you in particular!'

CHAPTER TEN

KIRSTEN found that Peter was little trouble, despite his discomfort. He bore it stoically, clomping about on crutches. His presence went some way, she discovered, towards helping to dull the pain of her broken engagement.

Her thoughts had been tormented, her dreams semi-nightmares. Time and again she had, in her troubled sleep, confronted Scott with Lavinia's assertion. Repeatedly, in those dreams, he had denied them, told her it was her he loved, not her house, and she had begun to believe him, only to awaken and find reality hitting her for the thousandth time. *Of course he would tell her he loved her! He had so much to gain by making her believe it was the truth*.

Peter's firm sent him paperwork to do. He had begun to look forward to its arrival because, he said, it stopped him getting bored. But Kirsten guessed that it was for another reason.

The messenger came, every time, in the shape of a young attractive blonde, hands ring-free, expression sweet. She was, Peter told Kirsten, one of the new secretaries who had arrived during his absence. She left him, each time, with a dreamy smile on his face.

Three weeks later a bandage, firm and strong, replaced the plaster on his leg. He still used a stick for support. He had returned to work, Kirsten driving him there every day.

Collecting him one afternoon, she noticed an air

about him of news to impart, but he kept up the small talk until he was seated, with the usual cup of tea, in an armchair.

'Heard of Samsom Developments?'

Kirsten caught her breath. 'You know I have. What about them? What are they after now?'

'One of their top men rang us. He wants us to draw up plans for the residential development of Hazel Farm.'

'No!' she whispered, unbelieving. 'Scott told me he hadn't sold the farm.'

'At the time, maybe he hadn't. Or he could have lied.'

'Scott wouldn't lie—would he?' But hadn't he acted out a lie in proposing marriage, calling her 'my love' and making passionate love? It had all been one terrible untruth—to get half-possession of her house, then win her over to part with the entire building to him, intending all along to do his worst—demolish it!

'Maybe,' Peter went on—did his eyes hold a tinge of pity? 'even then he had plans to develop it himself.'

'What do you mean by that?' asked Kirsten hoarsely.

Peter put down his cup and saucer. 'I've discovered his little secret. He's one of the directors of Samson Developments.'

Kirsten felt ill, her face draining, her eyelids lowering in an effort to shut out what was almost certainly the truth.

'You all right, pal?' Peter's gentle anxiety was almost her undoing, but she was too shocked for tears.

For some days she had been wondering if she had been right to accept Lavinia's statement at face value. Shouldn't she perhaps have given Scott a chance to clear himself? Shouldn't she have challenged him about the contents of Lennard Hazelton's secret letter?

Now all her doubts on that score were wiped away. Now she knew he was even guiltier of duplicity than she had assumed, more hypocritical, too; guilty, in addition, of subterfuge and trickery. When she had told him about the letters she had received from Samson, all he had said was that he knew the firm.

Why hadn't he told her the truth then—that he was behind the offers they had made, that he had, in fact, initiated them himself?

'At present,' Peter told her, 'it's just for outline planning permission—small dwellings, one-story, all of them.' Kirsten was too stunned to respond. 'You can see the plans at the council offices. Any member of the public has the right to view them.'

'I'll take your word for it, Peter.'

He smiled understandingly. 'If you feel like screaming, go ahead. That guy has let you down so badly——'

She shot to her feet. 'I'm going to see him. Tomorrow I'll go to London and burst into his office——'

'Without an appointment,' Peter cautioned, 'they wouldn't let you within a mile of him.'

Kirsten stared at Scott's ring. When the time was right from her point of view, she would remove it. Until then, why shouldn't she use its presence on her finger?

'I could wave this in front of the security men's noses.'

'They'd ring him through,' he pointed out, 'ask if he was expecting his fiancée. Suppose he said, "What fiancée?" You'd feel like that.' He put a tiny gap between forefinger and thumb.

The way Scott had treated her, she could believe anything of him.

'So I'll ring for an appointment.' She consulted her watch. 'He might still be there.' Peter was shaking his head as she went to the telephone.

'I'm sorry, Miss Ingram,' the secretary replied,

'but Mr Baird left some while ago. He usually leaves an address, but this time he didn't. So sorry.' She actually sounded it, Kirsten thought sadly.'

'Tomorrow,' she said to Peter next day, 'your parents are coming home. I don't want you to think I'm turning you out, but——'

'You're telling me where the exit door is.' He made a face. 'I guess you're right. If I stay here after they get back, tongues will start wagging.'

Mid-morning, Kirsten and Peter drank their coffee on the stone terrace. Mostly, they talked about Peter's work. Kirsten went along with it to try and keep her mind from her problems.

Memories of their relationship, hers and Scott's, of their coming together—although it had all been a wicked pretence on his part—were still overpoweringly strong in her mind. She had loved him so. Yet, now she hated him with an ache that was tearing her apart.

Peter snapped his fingers and she jumped out of her trance.

'I can imagine where your thoughts were. I suppose I haven't stood a chance, have I?'

'Come on,' she teased, 'you know there's another woman in your life. Name of Tessa?'

He coloured. 'She's just about noticing me,' he agreed. 'I think my condition,' he indicated his legs, 'has touched her heart, if nothing else.

Cutting across their conversation, there came from the near-distance a sound that turned Kirsten cold. It resembled that of a key turning. It was surely her imagination, wasn't it? But Peter had heard it too.

'Your friendly neighbourhood burglar?' he suggested. 'Gentlemanlike, using a key to the front door?'

Then the penny dropped. Peter's mouth fell open. It

wasn't, Kirsten reasoned frantically, it couldn't be! Scott had finished with her, he'd said. She had slowly been accepting the fact that, love him or hate him, she would never see him again. But she had forgotten that he was still her tenant and had paid the rent for six months in advance!

She leapt to her feet, racing through the house. He had reached the foot of the stairs. Two freezing brown eyes regarded her. Her colour was high, her breathing near to panting.

'You can't come here,' she told him, decisiveness prevailing over secretly trembling limbs. 'You must go at once. From this moment, I'm cancelling the agreement I made with you. I'm ending your tenancy.'

That ridged jaw she had once trailed her fingers along hardened until it began to resemble granite. Those brown eyes that had, in another lifetime, stroked her body all over now seared burning trails across her, singeing her flesh.

Scott put down his case and slipped his hands into his trouser pockets, the jacket of his suit draping over them. He must have gone there straight from his office. He was businessman personified, every single inch of him.

His fine sensual mouth was compressed into a scarlet line. 'That contract we signed,' he said, each word steel sparking off steel, 'was drawn up correctly and legally by a lawyer of our mutual choice—Mr Phipps, no less. Signed by you, signed by me. It would stand up to examination in any court of law. And,' he moved step by step towards her, 'if you so much as lay one destructive finger on a single page of it, I'll drag you through the courts by every means I know, without mercy. If necessary, until I drain you of every penny you possess.'

She had gone cold again, was shivering inside. Yet her

head went back and she countered, 'Yes, that would be one way of getting your hands on my house, wouldn't it, forcing me to sell—to you—so as to pay damages and costs, and heaven knows what else? Leaving me homeless, as well as penniless—not that you'd care!'

Scott's eyebrows rose, slowly and reducingly. 'If you've changed your mind and want to sell, my offer still stands. I might even offer you an alternative home—with me. Without the benefit of marriage, of course. I'm through with that.'

'Why, you——' Her hand lifted, but he caught it, his hold bruising and merciless, making her lower lip tremble.

He felt the ring on her finger, turning her arm so that he could examine it. 'Who are you wearing that for? Myself? In which case, I demand everything that goes with being your fiancé. Or is it your boyfriend? Couldn't he afford the outlay, so you said to him, let's use this?'

'Peter would never——' Kirsten checked herself, seeing the flash of fury. 'He's not my boyfriend! Understand?' How clever he was—he'd put her on the defensive.

'Hey, pet,' Peter called with just a touch of petulance, 'what's keeping you? I'm feeling lonely without you.'

Kirsten could not prevent the colour from sweeping over her. Peter had deliberately provoked, probably thinking he was helping her.

'He's a permanent fixture, then?' Scott dropped her wrist. 'Clever fellow! And without marriage too. You might be wearing the ring I bought you, but I've never managed to get that far into your life.' He retrieved his luggage, climbing the stairs.

'Whew!' Peter pretended to mop his brow. 'That was

some battle! I can't quite fix on the winner, though. You look slightly bruised, but I bet he doesn't have one scratch mark. Next time, Kirsten pet, put those claws of yours to better use—brand him for life.' Then he saw her trembling lips and covered her hand with his. 'Reaction, shock, that's all. Tell yourself he's a first-class swine, that all your feeling for him's dead. Yes?'

She nodded, mopping her eyes and choking back the sobs.

It was later, as she cooked lunch, that she saw Scott again. He stood in the doorway. Her movements grew jerky and she dropped a saucepan, furious with herself for doing such a thing under his cool scrutiny.

He was dressed in a navy cotton shirt, unbuttoned at the throat, and blue denims that followed faithfully his broad hips and taut thighs. The mere sight of him stirred her emotions—worse, her desire for his touch.

Unable to stand his disinterested appraisal, she queried in a freezing tone, her cheeks perversely growing heated, 'Is there something you want?'

'I notice there's been minimal progress with the repairs and renovations. Has Fred Burns lost his assistant?'

Didn't he realise, Kirsten thought, that that was a centenarian's lifetime ago?

Steeling herself for the explosion, she answered, 'I told him not to come any more. I couldn't afford to pay.'

'I was the one who was footing the bill!' The icy flash of the eyes, the arctic tone—they were worse than a volcanic eruption.

'Past tense, Scott,' she answered crisply, sounding as calm as a summer's day, but experiencing a typhoon deep inside. Would she *never* get him out of her system? 'The only hold you have on Tall Trees now is the leasing of two or three rooms. And I'd get you out of those if I possibly could.'

Her back was to him, and she heard him move, felt him behind her, his body making tantalisingly close contact with hers. His breath made the skin of her neck prickle. At once, her bodily responses came alive at his proximity. Her heart was pounding at the thought that he might touch her, pull her round, hold her . . . One finger on her, one hint of a softening of those glacial eyes and she'd be lost . . .

Then he was gone, and she collapsed, head lowered, arms dangling, against the kitchen units. A few minutes later she heard the sound of bricks being loaded, sand being shovelled, a wheelbarrow trundling. Scott was working on her house, and there was nothing she could—or dared—do about it!

At lunch time he disappeared, and Kirsten guessed he had gone to the Three White Horses. She ate her meal with Peter at the kitchen table, where he had more room to stretch his still-bandaged legs.

When Scott returned, Kirsten recognised Fred Burns' voice. Tommy was there too, whistling just like old times.

Scott swept through the house when the afternoon was over, striding through the kitchen where the aroma of the evening meal lingered appetisingly.

'Scott?' He paused. 'There's enough here for you to share——'

'Thanks, but no. I have a date—at the Moated Castle.'

It was as well, Kirsten thought, that he hadn't turned round. He would have seen the extreme distress in her face turning to stark, excruciating jealousy.

Kirsten was kneeling down and helping Peter remove his shoes as he sat on the bed late that evening, when

Scott returned. He stood in the doorway, eyes cutting into her crouching figure, contempt in every angle of his features.

'Will you tell me where I can find some towels?'

In his evening suit and black tie he looked devastating, his broad shoulders filling out the jacket, his height reducing that of the doorway that framed him.

'I'm sorry.' She straightened, flustered, brushing back her hair, wishing she had thought to change into a dress. But she told herself she could be wearing the most glamorous outfit she could find, and he would still be looking at her as if she had crawled out of a sack of potatoes. 'They're in the cupboard in the bathroom. I'll——'

'Stay where you are. The last thing I want to do is to ruin the atmosphere for the great love scene!'

She ran after him, hurling at his climbing figure, 'So how was *your* date, then? Did she say "no" when you invited her back, in spite of the fantastic meal you treated her to?' Then she swept back into Peter's bedroom.

Peter left next morning, Kirsten taking him and his belongings in her car. Returning home, she found that Scott was working outside. This time he was alone, the builders having taken the day off.

When she called out to him, asking whether he intended taking a coffee break, he answered, icily polite and without looking up, 'Would you bring it out here, please?'

Two, she thought, can play at that game. 'Your coffee,' she snapped, placing the mug on an upturned wooden box. As she turned to go, a hand on her arm detained her.

Standing rigidly, almost holding her breath, she waited for his hand to move. 'There was no need,' he said, 'to send your boyfriend away just because I'm here.' Far from releasing her, his hold tightened and he swung her round. 'Don't use me as a whipping boy as a release for your frustrations and sense of deprivation!'

Struggling, Kirsten levered her arm free, at some pain to herself. Blazing-eyed, she stared up at him. 'First, and I repeat, Peter is *not* my boyfriend. He's a friend and a good one, but I love him like the brother I never had.' The sceptical eyebrows incensed her. 'Second, your presence here has no effect on me at all, so I wouldn't want to make use of you, would I? You're my tenant—no more, no less. Do you understand now?'

Scott's narrowed eyes and thrusting jaw told her that it would not have taken much more for him to have used force to quell her outburst. She shivered at the thought, feeling not anger as she should have done, but an excitement which frightened her with its intensity. Oh God, she thought, I still love this man, when I should be hating him for what he has done, and would dearly love to do, to my life.

Watching television in the living-room in the late afternoon, she heard him come in and climb the stairs. There was the sound of water running and she guessed he was taking a shower, preparatory, no doubt, to meeting his date again.

Her heart felt as if it had been torn out by the roots. Picturing him with another woman was almost as painful as actually seeing him with her. Had Lavinia Baird come out into the country in secret and booked into the Moated Castle while he stayed discreetly at Tall Trees?

Only partially absorbed in the film she watched, she pricked up her ears at the sound of movement.

Turning her head, she saw that Scott was watching the screen. No evening suit this time, but casual dark trousers and a crew-necked pullover over an open-necked shirt. So I've miscalculated, Kirsten thought, his date's later this evening.

Despite the antipathy she felt towards him, she was glad she had taken more trouble with her appearance, choosing a slender-fitting, round-necked dress, her arms bare, her waist caught by a tie belt. She had used a little make-up too, emphasising her large eyes and filling in her wide, attractive mouth.

Scott moved to the window, staring out.

'Please sit down,' she invited impersonally. 'It's quite a good film, and——'

He swung round, hands in pockets, approaching. 'If you don't stop,' he ground between his teeth, 'playing the ever-helpful landlady, I'll throttle you with these,' he held up his hands, 'until you cry for mercy!'

Kirsten folded her arms, hiding her tight fists under them. 'I was only——'

He reached down and gripped her upper arms, hauling her to her feet. 'Now tell me why you ran out on me. If it wasn't for love of your tame architect——'

'Peter had an accident,' she answered, her voice low. Scott released her and she rubbed her bruised arms. 'He swerved to avoid a lorry in a narrow road and his car rolled down the verge. His legs were fairly badly injured.'

He was listening, face inscrutable.

'His parents were abroad, so I was the only person he could turn to. He's been here ever since. Now do you believe me? He's got more than a passing interest in a new secretary at work.'

'Which upsets you?'

'Why should it?' There was no more understanding in

him now than before. But why should it worry her? He had behaved so badly towards her in so many ways, what he thought of her shouldn't matter any more. And it didn't, she told herself, it didn't!

Feeling that the only way to put a safe distance between them was to get out of the room, she made for the door, but something checked her progress. It could have been the strength of his mind, or some strange power Scott had over her.

Storm in her eyes, she blurted out, 'Peter told me what you're intending to do. How could you? How could you have lied to me about Hazel Farm? You did sell it, didn't you? And to Samson Developments.'

His eyebrows formed imperious arches. 'I did? That's news.'

'So if it's not them, who's applying for planning permission to build houses just beyond the orchard—your orchard—and which you'll no doubt destroy, then sell for house-building there, too?'

'I am.'

'*You* are? But someone from Samson Developments rang Peter's firm!' she exclaimed.

'A friend of mine. I asked him to as a favour. I was abroad.'

Kirsten went up to him, her face white now with disbelief and bitterness. 'So you, who asked me to be your wife—you cared so little for my wishes that you've been planning all the time, coldly and deliberately, to do what you know I've been dreading ever since I inherited this place? *You* are going to surround Tall Trees with bricks and mortar?'

Scott made no response, steadily holding her gaze.

She would shake him somehow. 'And I know something else about you too.'

'You do?' His tone held amused interest, and she

wanted to hit him.

'Something Peter told me he had heard in the course of his work. Something that makes you guilty of duplicity and double-dealing. *I know that you're one of the directors of Samson Developments.*'

'So?'

'So when I told you soon after we'd met that Samson had written to me offering to buy this house, you should have told me then.'

'Like hell I should! What business was it of yours what my directorships connected me with? I'm a busy man, as you may have guessed in our short acquaintance. Which means I can't keep up with every twist and turn of thought of the companies in which I hold those directorships. Somehow they must have heard about my great-uncle's death. He was well known in the business world, as you must know. He still kept up his City contacts, despite his great age.'

All this was so true, it disconcerted her. But only for a moment. 'You sound plausible, Scott, and believable. But nothing can take away what you're doing with Hazel Farm.'

'Determined to attack me on every side, aren't you? A man can dispose as he likes of his property.' He looked her over. 'There's no connection between us now. Maybe we were lovers—on one occasion. You were not the only woman in my life.'

Every statement he made was calculated to target her, like thrown knives around a woman at a fair. But this man's knives hit her, each one drawing blood and pain and inner tears. And almost killing her.

'I know why you wanted to marry me,' she cried. 'To cover your affair with your brother's wife. She might have married Larry, but she never gave you up, nor you her. I know you denied wanting her any more, but that was only to trick me into accepting your proposal of marriage. And I know another reason why you wanted me as your wife!'

'I'm learning things about myself this afternoon,' drawled Scott, 'that I never knew before. So tell me that other reason.' His eyes grew ruthless, deliberately sensual, moving over her body inch by inch, making her feel as if he were stripping her naked. 'There are the usual ones, of course, that attracts a man to any woman.'

So he was reducing her to the level of 'any woman', was he?

'You wanted Tall Trees, that's why,' she accused. 'It was the only way you could think of to get it. I'd refused your offers to buy the house, so you tried other ways to get your hands on the property!'

Scott stared inscrutably into her face, and she felt she was making no impression on his conscience.

'You proposed to me, bought me jewellery, planned an allowance for me, plus diverting to me income from the estate. You bought the library to give me financial help. It was so *generous* of you, wasn't it? But it wasn't generosity, it was bribery. All the time, you were coercing me—by then you calculated I'd be your "devoted wife"—into allowing you to take over Tall Trees within our marriage. Then you could do whatever you liked with it without a whimper of protest from me!'

Scott walked away, staring through the window into the garden.

'Quite a list,' he said at last. 'Quite an indictment.'

'Even if you wanted to, you couldn't deny your interest in Tall Trees was linked with your proposal to me.'

'Go on.'

'There was a letter—Mr Hazelton's letter, the one he left for you to read after he'd died.' He was listening intently now. 'It said, and I quote, "If you want the house, you'll have to marry the girl." Now tell me I'm wrong.'

'Who told you this,' he asked stonily, 'Mr Phipps?'

'Lavinia Baird told me, your woman—your mistress! That's who told me.'

'So what else did my *mistress*, as you call her, tell you about my great-uncle's letter?'

'Nothing. There was nothing to tell.'

His brows lifted in response. 'Tell me something. Why should it worry you what's built in the environs of this house, when you plan to convert it into retirement apartments?'

Kirsten stared down at her clasped hands.

'That was just a dream. It'll never come true. I haven't even got the capital to start planning, let alone do anything practical towards achieving it.'

'Kirsten?' He was near enough for her to touch him now, if things had been different. If she looked up at him as he obviously wanted, she would give everything away—her sadness at the breaking of their engagement; Scott's continued involvement with the woman from his past. He would see how much she still loved him. And how hopelessly.

His finger tipped her face. 'If I told you my plans for the Hazel Farm development . . . if I told you I intend to build retirement homes on that land, how would you feel about it then?'

The look in her eyes was like the sun coming through after thick mist clearing.

'With every modern facility,' he went on, 'with wardens on round-the-clock duty, with electronic equipment like personal alarms and intercom, medical attention whenever needed, communal eating facilities as an alternative to eating alone?'

He was smiling now at the radiance of her expression. 'With a room for social evenings, a gymnasium, a swimming pool for exercise? And anything else that anyone can think of to help senior citizens grow older with dignity and in the very best of health? How would you feel then?'

Now she could not stop the tears, they ran down her cheeks, even as her eyes shone like stars.

'Would you,' asked Scott, 'call it bribery on my part, wanting to "soften" you into accepting my offer to buy Tall Trees?'

Kirsten tried to speak through tremulous lips. Her hands reached up to rest on his chest, but she drew them away quickly. He was not hers to touch at will any more. She had put him out of her life and, despite this wonderful gesture on his part, she must never forget he was a businessman through and through. And he had shown no positive signs of wanting her back in his life.

Moving away, she started pulling absently at the engagement ring. She gazed at him with open admiration for the plans he had placed before her. 'It would make me very happy, Scott, to see that come about. And I know Mr Hazelton would have been proud to hear what you intend to do. That way, you can mix philanthropy and altruism with good business practice. It should bring you in a great deal of money——'

Scott's jaw clamped shut. 'Money and business be damned!' He gripped her shoulders and half shook her. 'Will you stop denigrating every single good idea I have, every positive action I take? You seem to take a fiendish pleasure in attributing every well-intentioned thing I do to selfish motives on my part.'

'Is that what it looks like? It's not true, Scott. It's only that——' a sigh came from her depths '—that from the moment you showed such interest in buying this house, I've been on the defensive where you're concerned.' She gazed at him. 'Will you tell me something? Why were you so keen to buy my home?'

His wide shoulders shrugged. 'At first glance, demolition was all it seemed fit for. But on second thoughts, and hearing your defence of it—and your love of it,' he added enigmatically, 'I realised it would be possible to save it, to revive it with renovations and repairs. I decided I wanted Tall Trees to go on living.'

She nodded. It was wonderful to hear him talk that way. 'I'm sorry about my accusations, and for misjudging you so badly. But you must admit the cards were stacked against my doing anything else. Now——' she tugged harder and the ring came off '—I only kept this on for the sake of appearances, to let people think we'd drifted apart slowly.'

He took the ring. 'Drifted apart? To hell with that!' With an angry movement he seized her hand and pushed the ring back into place. 'That's where it belongs and that's where it will stay.' She frowned, puzzled by his action. 'Did you really think I'd let the only woman I've ever truly loved go out of my life? And without a fight?'

Kirsten's lips parted. 'You mean, you love me?'

'For God's sake, woman—I more than love you. I live and breathe you! You're part of me, Kirsten. Come, my love,' he whispered, 'for the sake of my sanity, my peace of mind, come to me, darling.'

His arms opened wide. She stared at the space, then ran into it. It closed around her, his mouth moving hungrily over her. He tipped her face and kissed her eyes, her throat, her nose and then her mouth with a thrust of possession that left her weak with happiness.

'Scott darling,' she encircled his waist with her arms, 'I don't know how I've lived all these weeks away from you. I haven't lived, I've existed.'

'And how do you think I've felt? How I felt when the woman I love left me high and dry?'

Like her limbs, her eyes were melting, telling him a secret that made him catch his breath.

He swung her into his arms and carried her upstairs, into his room and on to the wide bed. With love and controlled desire, he undressed her, kissing each and every part of her as it was exposed to his fierce, male gaze. With each look he was taking her into him, and moments later, when they lay naked together, he made caressing love to her, joining with her urgent, arching body and climbing with her to the summit of shared, fulfilled desire.

'I never thought,' she said later, her voice muffled against his chest, 'that I'd find such happiness again. You're the only man I've ever wanted to share my life with. But,' her head lifted, 'you know that, don't you?'

'We-ll,' Scott teased, 'whatever happened to that woman who couldn't take my life-style? Or that pet cat that felt the urge to revert to the wild and sink her claws into everything in sight?'

Kirsten laughed, then coloured. He kissed her blushing breasts and fiery cheeks, and even redder, pouting mouth, still full and moist from his attentions.

'I had to hit back at you somehow,' she explained, 'after what your sister-in-law told me. Considering everything else that had happened, it didn't seem unreasonable to believe her.' She paused. 'Did she really see the letter?'

'By accident, one day when she strayed into my study. It was lying on the desk, and she took it out of the envelope.'

Her fingers made whorls in his chest hair. 'Was it true what she told me—that your great-uncle wrote that you would have to marry me to get the house?'

'It was.'

She stiffened. She could not, would not believe it!

'But it said a lot more. So you can stop going frigid on me, Miss Ingram,' Scott shifted her so that her body was on top of his, 'and hear what else my great-uncle said. He said,' he reached up and kissed her mouth, 'that I'd be a clever man indeed if I could budge you on the subject of Tall Trees. That you'd never part with it, not even if I were lucky enough to get you to agree to marry me. That you'd stick to your plans come hell or high water. And that he wished me all the luck in the world in getting you to say "yes"—to me as a husband. And, Miss Ingram," he tweaked her nose, 'from the moment I saw you that day as you sat at your desk, with the sunlight on your hair, I knew you were the only woman I'd ever love, whether you married me or not.'

Kirsten looked down at him, her smile radiant. 'If only I'd known the truth! It would have saved so much misery.'

'For me as well as you.'

'But I was sure that, deep down, you were still in love with Lavinia.'

'Good grief, whatever gave you that impression?' he exclaimed.

'The way she kept you with her at the party. You didn't do much to prise yourself away. Nor did you tell me about her, as I thought you would if you'd really got her out of your system.'

'She was never in it. Until you, no woman has been, and you, my love, are in my bloodstream, part of me, as essential to my continued living as my heart is. And now I want you to be part of me again.'

Later, they stood on the terrace, arms round each other, each other's face reflecting the glorious colours of the sunset.

'You had a date last night,' Kirsten mentioned in a falsely casual tone. 'What was her name?'

Scott's laughter rang out. 'If you must know, Philip Phipps.'

She stiffened. 'Oh? Why?'

'Now come on,' he urged, 'soften up again. Haven't I laid your suspicions and doubts to rest yet?' She smiled. 'That's better. It was about the Hazel Farm development. Do you want the boring details now or later?'

She shook her head, laughing. 'And do you have a date for tonight?'

Scott clicked his fingers as though he had forgotten, 'You're right—I must change. I've booked a table at the Moated Castle.'

Her face straightened, then, determined to keep her doubts down where they belonged, she asked, 'What time will you be back?'

'That depends on how late my date keeps me out. She and I will be celebrating—this time alone, without a party to keep us apart.'

'What's her name, this date?'

'We-ll, at the moment it's——' he kissed her nose and then her willing lips, 'Kirsten Ingram, but before the month is out it'll be Baird, Mrs Scott Baird.' His mouth rooted for her ear. 'Will you like that, my love?'

'I can't wait,' she whispered, 'for that moment to come.'

His arms around her roughened as he pulled her closer. 'You won't have to, my darling,' he murmered, 'you won't have to. Not now, nor ever again.'

A toast to the newcomers!

This is a unique collection of four new and exciting novels which have been carefully selected from over 5,000 manuscripts submitted by novelists who've never before appeared in paperback.

We're sure Jacqueline Baird, Deborah Davis, Michelle Reid and Lee Wilkinson are destined to join our ranks of best selling Romance writers, whom everyone will come to know and love in future years.

Price £4.80   Published April 1988

Mills & Boon

Available from Boots, Martins, John Menzies, W. H. Smith, Woolworths and other paperback stockists.

Conscience, scandal and desire.

A dynamic story of a woman whose integrity, both personal and professional, is compromised by the intrigue that surrounds her.

Against a background of corrupt Chinese government officials, the CIA and a high powered international art scandal, Lindsay Danner becomes the perfect pawn in a deadly game. Only ex-CIA hit man Catlin can ensure she succeeds... and lives.

Together they find a love which will unite them and overcome the impossible odds they face.

Available May. Price £3.50

W●RLDWIDE

Available from Boots, Martins, John Menzies, W.H. Smith, Woolworths and other paperback stockists.

Mills & Boon
COMPETITION

How would you like a
year's supply of Mills & Boon Romances
ABSOLUTELY FREE?
Well, you can win them! All you have to do is complete the word
puzzle below and send it into us by 30th June 1988
The first five correct entries picked out of the bag after that date
will each win a year's supply of Mills & Boon Romances (Ten
books every month – worth over £100!) What could be easier?

```
S L O V E S O R M I R P
N E P U C R E T T U B A
O E L B Y P P O P L S N
W O A K L U P I N O U S
D M V C C S L R W C C Y
R I E T O U H I M A O A
O T N I T W S S L L R I
P E D D A I S Y L I C L
S L E A N D B L E L E H
O O R C H I D O I N S A
L I L Y A L O I V P O D
N V L I D O F F A D R H
```

Lavender	Rose	Primrose	Cowslip
Honeysuckle	Tulip	Snowdrop	Lilac
Buttercup	Iris	Orchid	Lupin
Crocus	Daisy	Dahlia	
Poppy	Violet	Pansy	**PLEASE TURN**
Daffodil	Viola	Lily	**OVER FOR**
			DETAILS
			ON HOW
			TO ENTER

How to enter

All the words listed overleaf, below the word puzzle, are hidden in the grid. You can find them by reading the letters forwards, backwards, up or down, or diagonally. When you find a word, circle it, or put a line through it. After you have found all the words, the left-over letters will spell a secret message that you can read from left to right, from the top of the puzzle through to the bottom.

Don't forget to fill in your name and address in the space provided and pop this page in an envelope (you don't need a stamp) and post it today. Hurry – competition ends 30th June 1988

Only one entry per household please.

Mills & Boon Competition,
FREEPOST,
P.O. Box 236,
Croydon,
Surrey CR9 9EL.

Secret message _____

_____

Name_____

Address_____

_____

_____

_____Postcode_____

COMP 4